Unraveling

Unraveling

Allegra Craver

Unraveling
Copyright © 2019 Allegra Craver

Content Editor: Abigail Mechley
Copy Editor: Catherine Lynch
Editor-in-Chief: Kristi King-Morgan
Formatting: Kristi King-Morgan
Cover Photography: Thomas Vielkind
Cover Concept: Christopher Freeman
Cover Design and Graphics: Krisnina Magpantay

ISBN: 978-1-947381-21-6

Dreaming Big Publications
www.dreamingbigpublications.com

Dedicated to my wonderful family, without whom I'd be lost.

1

Okay Brooklyn, you can do it. Just breathe in and out.

"Brooklyn Perce?" My head snaps to the spindly woman standing in the doorway looking at her clipboard over her massive glasses. I stand up and smooth out the dress I bought a day ago specifically for this purpose. The same goes for the lipstick I'm wearing and the boots I have on. I've been waiting for this day for my entire life. There's no way I'm going into that interview room dressed like a slob. "This way, please."

I calmly follow the woman down the long cinderblock hallway while trying to stand up straight. My breathing still won't follow a regular pattern, so I try to force it to. It doesn't work. My heart won't stop vigorously beating either. Nerves, I suppose. The woman opens a door and holds it open, smiling encouragingly.

"Good luck," she says. I nod and swallow as she closes the door behind me.

The office I'm standing in looks like something out of the Pottery Barn catalogues my mom receives in the mail at home. A mahogany desk is complemented with a padded leather chair and one of those small green desk lamps every corporate bigwig seems to have. Two tall mahogany shelves stacked with books and VHS tapes are flanking the window that looks out over the entire campus. I try not to get distracted by the beautiful warm sun shining in the window as I smile at the man behind the desk.

"Hello Sir. Nice to meet you. I'm Brooklyn Perce." I offer my hand to shake, and he takes it. His grip is unsurprisingly strong.

"Hello Brooklyn. Have a seat." I bite my lip and quickly sit down in one of the two massive leather chairs in front of his desk. The man has greying hair which is thinning on the crown of his head. He's wearing a collared shirt with a patterned sweater vest over it. The Rolex watch on his right wrist catches the sunlight as it glares at me. I suddenly feel small as the weight of the situation sinks in. "Are you enjoying Resslar?"

"Yes, very much. I've wanted to go to RU since I was a kid and being here is like a dream come true. I've always wanted to work in radio, and I think WRDW might be a great place to start since I've worked at a station before and it was really—" *Crap, I'm rambling.* I look down and smooth my dress as I give myself a chance to breathe. "It was a fantastic experience." I clear my throat and look at him encouragingly, waiting for the first question. My leg shakes as I try to give the passing appearance of calmness by folding my hands on my lap.

"Fantastic. Glad you're enjoying campus. You can call me Peter, by the way. So, let's get right to it. Why do you want to work for WRDW?" Peter asks in his short tone.

"I've wanted to work in the radio industry ever since I was young. In fact, I listened to WRDW as a kid! I just love the idea of informing people, especially in such a classic format. I think most kids don't realize that the first TV shows were inspired by existing radio shows. Like, soap operas started on radio then went to TV when the medium fell somewhat out of favor." Peter nods and makes a note on my resume. *Yes. He liked that answer.* I sit up a little straighter. My leg stops shaking.

"Why did you listen growing up? Do you leave close to here?" asks Peter.

"About an hour south in New Jersey. My parents always had the WRDW station on in the car and as I got older, I appreciated the mix of music and talk, but I've always had a love for the news. I have, like, four news apps on my phone just so I can cross-reference them with one another. Each source has a different political bent on most things, so it's always good to be informed regarding what each side is thinking. I covered the general election for my high school paper and just had CNN, NBC, Fox, FiveThirtyEight, and CBS on a loop." Peter snorts, a little smile growing on his face. I smile at how ridiculous that must have sounded. "I know, it seems crazy."

"It's always good to be informed. Half the guys in the newsroom right now don't know their ass from their elbow." He looks up at me from my resume, clearly thinking about something by the way he chews a little on his bottom lip. "You have some impressive experience, Brooklyn. I mean, interning at local radio stations since freshman year of high school? That's commitment I don't normally see."

"I knew what I wanted to do," I say honestly. Peter scoots his chair closer to his desk, coming up from his laid-back position so he can put his hands on the tabletop.

"What did you do for the stations?"

"I went out on assignments either alone or in a team—"

"So you've had experience reporting in pairs?" Once I nod, Peter nods back approvingly. "Good to know."

My back is as straight as it's ever been as I try to contain my smile. "And I reported on everything from pet shelters to student government to the mayoral election. I also played music, but that was once or twice. I was just filling in." Peter scribbles something down on my resume.

"And you're aware that this isn't a paid position, correct?" he asks.

"Absolutely. Just doing it for the love of broadcasting," I half-heartedly joke, letting a contained smile crack my face.

"That's what I like to hear." Peter folds his hands on the table and looks down at my resume, nodding. "Tell you what. You're clearly one of the most qualified candidates in that room. Now, since you're a first-semester freshman you're going to be working sporadically. Let's start with you writing a couple of local news stories. We'll have you transcribe interviews and write broadcast scripts to be read on air. This, of course, is all on deadline." He raises his eyebrows. "Think you can handle that?"

"Of course," I say reassuringly, practically bouncing in my seat.

"While I get the paperwork squared away, we can give you a tour of the station, make sure you're familiar with the audio editing software and all of that. Maybe if you show some promise in these first two or three weeks, I'll see if we can get you more stories." Peter's mouth makes a little smile. "What do you say?"

"Yes!" I try not to burst. I jump up from the chair and try to contain my smile. "That sounds fantastic. Thank you so much Sir!"

"Peter," he corrects. "I'll be in touch. Have a great day."

I skip down the hall and sprint out of the front door before I let myself throw a fit of happiness.

✷ ✷ ✷

"Hey, hey, hey!" I exclaim with joy as I sit down in the bustling dining hall. Drew slurps her soup and flicks her eyes up to me through her worn dyed navy-blue hair. My roommate puts down her spoon and sips her cup of soda.

"Hey what's up?" she says. I relax back into my seat and put my hands behind my head, looking out one of the many floor-to-ceiling windows. There are kids outside walking to and from class chatting with their friends. They seem like they're having a great time and why shouldn't they be? It's one of the first nice days in a while since the October rains have decided to take a break. But I can guarantee none of them are as happy as I am right now.

"Oh nothing. You're just looking at the newest writer for WRDW!" Drew immediately brightens up. Her face breaks into a massive smile.

"Dude, that's amazing! Congrats!" my roommate exclaims. Kennedy sits down next to Drew, putting down her plate of food, pushing her black braids behind her shoulders as she prepares to dig in. Kennedy, Kenni for short, is a political science major and lives off coffee like most college kids so, of course, her lunch today includes a cup of the dining hall's finest. Luckily, she's not planning on going to law school which, I assume, would involve doubling the amount of coffee she drinks.

"What's amazing?" Kenni yawns, taking a swig from her mug.

"Brook is gonna be on WRDW!" Drew says.

"That's fantastic! Practically no one gets on the staff as a freshman! They must've really liked you," Kenni says.

"I'm so excited. This is a dream come true. I still can't believe this is happening," I chatter, bouncing in my seat.

"Hey Kenni, I think Brook has had more caffeine than you this morning," Drew jokes, nodding at my movement.

"Impossible. I've had four cups already and it's not even noon," Kenni says dryly, taking another sip from her massive mug. She looks at her phone and raises her eyebrow. "Oh would you look at that? It *is* noon" I snort as she shrugs and puts the phone down. "12:15 actually."

"Four cups before noon on a Monday? Is that a new record?" I tease her.

"Probably," Kenni confirms.

"Seriously though Brook, that's really amazing. When are you gonna be on the air?" Drew asks, intrigued. I shrug, stealing the bread roll off of her tray.

"Well, I'm not going to be *on air*. I'm going to write stories for the person who will read them on air. Peter said I'm going to write local stories at first before he gives me the national stuff," I explain in between bites of bread.

"Who's Peter?" asks Kenni, taking a bite of her salad, some of which falls out of the bowl it's in. A few tree nuts go rolling across the table, but no one does anything to stop them from falling.

"He's the adult station manager," I clarify. Kenni sighs wistfully.

"I wish I had time to do something cool like that. Half of the time, I'm being bombarded by either Chinese or policy studies and the other half, I'm trying to study in between naps," Kenni groans, flipping through the binder next to her. When I look at it, I see theories and laws that swim in my eyes.

"I wish I had your brain, dude. My mind can't even begin to comprehend that sort of thing." I finish the roll that I took from Drew and look at my phone for the time. "Ugh, I have class in an hour."

"That blows. You know who doesn't have class today?" Drew brags.

"Let me guess. You?" As an Art major, my roommate has five classes. Ever since she dropped a Philosophy class, she's had more time on her hands than ever thanks to her AP credits helping her out. Frankly, I envy her down time and I know Kenni does too.

"Yep!" Drew chirps, slurping more of her noodle soup.

"Lucky," Kenni groans. She angrily stabs at her salad which sends an almond flying across the table. "You want to hear something annoying?"

"Always," says Drew.

"My professor pronounced my name as 'Kay-nay-day' again today."

"Again? Seriously, you're named after one of the most famous presidents of the United States. It shouldn't be that hard," I say.

"Honestly, I hate my name. Just because my dad was obsessed with JFK means I now have to live with the name *Kennedy*."

"I think your name is pretty," Drew says, frowning.

"Thanks. At least you can pronounce it correctly, unlike my idiot of a Policy Studies professor," Kenni says. She looks at the phone and her eyes widen. "Shit, I have class in five. I'll see you guys later."

"Just as I was about to sit down," says a new voice. I look towards the head of the table and see Finn standing there, his tray loaded with about seven slices of pizza. Finn is sporting his typical outfit: a RU sweatshirt with jeans and worn sneakers. He looks sadly down at Kenni.

"Yeah I'm sorry. I have a recitation today." Kenni gives Finn a one-armed hug goodbye before she sticks an apple in her mouth and going towards the door.

"Bye Kay-nay-day!" Drew calls after her. Kenni pretends to laugh before rolling her eyes and running out of the dining hall. Finn watches her go and then takes her seat.

"Does she ever breathe?" he asks as he picks up his first slice.

"I don't really know," Drew responds. She looks over his face with care as he eats his food. "Hey, nice glasses. Are they new?" Finn's face lights up at Drew's comment. His bright blue eyes glisten behind the black frames as he looks at her.

"Yeah they are! Thanks for noticing."

"Well, they look good," she says.

"Thanks Drew. Hey Brook, how did that interview go?"

"I got the job!" I tell Finn, starting to bounce again.

"Wow! Congratulations!" Finn looks at me and puts his hand on my shoulder, holding me down from shaking excitedly in my seat. "Okay, see, that's what crazy people do. Stop bouncing."

"Sorry." I look out at the rest of the dining hall. It has filled up since I got here. Some students are sitting alone studying or on their phones, but mostly everyone is talking with their friends. I look at Drew who is starting lovingly at Finn as he devours his pizza like an animal. Deciding I'm not hungry, I pick up my bag and stand up.

"Hey, I'm going back to the room. I have to pick up a few things before class, and I have to call my mom. She's going to be so excited. I'll see you guys later," I say.

"Mmkay," Drew says dreamily.

"See you Brook!" Finn says, smiling at me. I wave good-bye to my friends and leave the dining hall through the tunnel.

Resslar University was built in the less than comfortable climate of Central New York. Since the winters are miserable, the school recently decided to build a tunnel from Rodgers Dining Hall to the two dorms on either side of it: Smith Hall, where Drew, Kenni, and I live, and Cypress Hall where Finn and his roommate live. I march up the stairs to the fourth floor of Smith, pass the elevator, go down a hallway, and stick my key into the sixth door down on the right.

Our dorm room is spectacularly decorated, my long wall being occupied with a huge mandala tapestry and the parallel wall decorated with pictures of Drew and her friends. The white rug is a bit fluffy underfoot, and the fairy lights going around the top of the room are always on. The floor is usually free of clutter as are the two desks. Posters of various movies and beach scenes are hanging on the wall parallel to the windows behind the TV. The entire vibe of the room calms me down when I'm feeling stressed.

I change out of my dress and into my favorite outfit: jeans and a blouse with ankle boots. I look at the clock on the microwave after I zip up my second brown boot and see it's a little after 12:30. I still have time before I have to walk to class, so I flop on my bed to call my mom and tell her about the interview. I quickly dial my mom's cell phone and wait through the beeping tone. She finally picks up.

"Hey honey. What's going on?"

"Hey Ma! Guess what?" I chirp.

"What?" my mom answers excitedly.

"I got the job at WRDW!" My mom screams of happiness, and I join her.

"Oh Brook, that's fantastic! I'm so proud of you!"

"Thank you! Yeah, the manager said I was one of the most qualified candidates in the room."

"See, I told you the high school radio station gig would pay off!"

"And I'm starting with writing local news, but he said if I show promise, he's going to give me more national stuff!"

"Brook, this is amazing. Seriously, I'm so proud of you." There's a pause. "Did you tell your father?"

"No, I didn't get to call Dad yet."

"Okay, well, call him and tell him. He'll be happy you have a job." My father is very into the idea of making it on your own, especially when it comes to making money. I'm guessing he won't be happy to

14

hear I'm not making anything from the station. Odds are, I probably won't call and will just tell him the next time I see him. "Is it getting cold up there?"

"Thankfully yes! I'm wearing boots right now."

"Oh, I bet you're even happier!"

I laugh. "Yes Ma, I am." I look at the clock again and see I have exactly five minutes to get to class on time. I spring up off of my bed, sling my bag over my shoulder, and speed walk out the door, leaving it unlocked for Drew under the assumption she'll be done with lunch soon. "How's home?"

"Everything's going well. I'm at work right now so ten different people want ten different things, but it's alright. I took Harley to the vet the other day and they said he's a bit bigger than is normal for a dog his size but if we cut back the amount of food we're giving him, he should be alright." I smile, thinking of my dog. Harley the Bernese mountain dog is the sweetest creature on Earth.

"Yeah, he doesn't need to be any bigger than he already is," I agree as I walk down the stairs in front of my building.

"Besides the new job, how's everything up there?" Ma asks.

"Pretty normal. The usual essay and test here and there, but nothing out of the ordinary." I think a little harder and then remember. "My food science class is kicking my ass a little bit with the amount of work, but I think I can handle it."

"If anyone can handle it, it's you. Any boys?"

I laugh and say dryly, "Yeah sure, they're busting down my door as we speak."

"Someone will come, Brooklyn. They'd be crazy not to."

"Well thank you, but you're my mom. You have to say that."

"I say it because it's true. Just keep your options open." There's a pause. "Oh shoot, my boss is calling for me. I have to go. I'll talk to you later honey! I love you so much!"

"I love you too! Bye!" I put my phone in the pocket of my bag before going into the lecture hall.

2

"Look who's late," Taylor mutters as I reluctantly slide into the only open seat next to him in COM134.

"Shut up," I whisper back. I quickly take out my laptop and open up a new Word document to take notes. The professor is lecturing about some advertising campaign related to our unit about PR. I'm majoring in broadcast journalism and to me, this lesson is pointless, but I have to listen anyway.

"You must *love* this lesson, Brooklyn," Taylor says. "It's right up your alley."

"Oh, I'm sorry, were you speaking?" I snap at him before looking off into the distance at the cute guy across the room. Taylor smirks, his cruel grey eyes sneering at me.

"He's out of your league, Perce," he jeers.

"You know him?" I try to say it casually, but I don't think it comes off that way because Taylor rolls his eyes.

"He's in my building. I don't know his name. Why don't you go over and ask him in front of the whole class?" he mocks.

"Excuse me!" The professor stops the entire lecture to pointedly stare at Taylor and me. All 50 heads turn towards us. I feel my face become hot and shift uncomfortably in my chair. Taylor, however, just looks innocently towards the professor. "Time to listen, yeah?"

17

"Yes Sir," Taylor says, trying to contain a snide tone. The professor nods before turning around, but even that doesn't stop Taylor from scoffing underneath his breath. "Way to go, Perce."

"Seriously, I don't think anyone would blame me if I just knocked you out cold," I say, shrugging and typing the words on the PowerPoint slideshow in front of me as the professor drones on.

"*Seriously* don't date outside your major, Brooklyn." I roll my eyes, but he continues. "You know, I would try to get with you if I wasn't in advertising. You're pretty hot." I turn to him quickly, fuming. Taylor, of course, laughs. His sharp features aren't at all softened by showing any sign of joy. "What?"

"I'm five seconds away from punching you in the nose," I tell him through clenched teeth. The advertising major has a hyena's smile.

"Do it. I dare you."

"Hey!" The kid in front of me turns around to confront Taylor and I have to look twice. He has kind amber eyes accented by dark brown hair and hard cheekbones. The blue shirt he has on makes the little flecks of green in his eyes pop. He looks at me and gives me a little smile. Taylor narrows his grey eyes, clearly angered.

"What?" he spits.

"The professor told you to shut up. She's got every right to punch you in the face, so stop talking and listen to the lecture." I give my hero a thankful smile, and he winks at me. The corner of Taylor's mouth is up in a snarl.

"This isn't your fight, man," he says.

The boy looks at him in disbelief. "Yeah it is if you won't stop after she's asked you to. Shut up and make something of your life by listening to the professor." Taylor looks like someone just slapped him as my hero turns back around. After glaring at me and grumbling something under his breath, Taylor stays silent for the rest of class.

*** *** ***

When the class is over, I try to catch up with the brown-haired boy, but I can't seem to find him. It's like he was never in class to begin with. I even look behind me to see if he somehow fell out of step with the rest of the mob, but there's no one resembling the boy who sat in front of me.

I leave the communications building in defeat and start the hike back to my dorm. On the way, I hear my phone ring from somewhere in the depths of my coat pocket. I rummage for it and finally see there is an unknown number calling me. Against my better judgement, I pick it up.

"Hello?" I ask tentatively.

"Is this Brooklyn Perce?" asks a man.

"Yes."

"Oh hey! I'm Ryker Williams, I'm the student manager of WRDW. I'm calling to confirm your schedule starting as soon as possible." I stop in my tracks in the middle of a sidewalk in the Quad, pull over onto the grass, drop my backpack onto the ground, and frantically search for my laptop to pull up my calendar. I get a few odd looks from the passing students, but once they notice I'm looking back at them, they glance away.

"Yeah, of course!" I say, zipping open the laptop sleeve. "Let me just get my computer."

"Got it?" Ryker asks. I tap the touchpad to wake my computer up and click the calendar icon when the display brightens.

"Yeah, I got it! Okay, what time would you like me to come in?"

"Whenever you're free. Sorry for the sudden start, by the way. Peter's really impressed by you apparently," says Ryker as I enter a new event in the calendar on my Mac. I smile to myself.

"I'm super excited to be working with you guys," I say, getting the same hyper feeling I felt earlier in the day.

"I'm excited too. I've never had an intern before." My eyebrows furrow.

"What?" I ask.

"Oh, yeah, you're going to be working with me!" Ryker says. My heart falls a bit, but then picks up again. "Don't worry, I won't treat you like an intern. Although if you run to The Coffee Bean before your shift, I will take advantage of that."

I laugh. "Of course. When do you want me to come in?"

"When do your classes end tomorrow?" asks Ryker.

"Noon," I say.

"Can you come in around one? Have lunch before. You're getting a tour and being trained tomorrow for an hour, and you need fuel," he advises.

"Sounds good!" I say as I type the name of the event into my Mac's calendar. "See you tomorrow?"

"Tomorrow. Your R.U.I.D. should get you into the station. If not, you have my number now so just give me a call."

"Okay! Bye!" I end the call and quickly stuff my laptop back into my bag, put the bag on my back, and tuck my hair behind my ear. I join the crowd of people and continue the walk back to my dorm.

I live on the highest point on campus which means I need to hike up or down several flights of stairs covered by a tunnel every time I want to go home. It makes getting to the top and then flopping onto my bed *that* much more gratifying. Once I get into my building and nod hello to everyone I see, I go up to my room and change into sweats and a t-shirt. I turn to Drew who's curled up on her bed in a blanket as she binge-watches *The Good Place*. "I'm going to do some laundry," I tell her, as I grab my massive black bag of dirty clothes and sling it over my shoulder. I also remember to grab the bottle of detergent from the top shelf of my closet. Drew gives me a thumbs up before I turn around and leave the room again.

The laundry room of Smith is buried deep in the basement of the building. The first time I found it, I thought I was in a place I shouldn't have been due to the exposed pipes and concrete floors but, the smell of detergent and dryer sheets was too overpowering to miss. I go to the second row of washers, dump my clothing out onto the top of a washer, and start to unceremoniously shove everything into the opening. When I was home, my mom taught me that laundry should have dark loads and light loads, but in college, everything goes in together. I'm about to finish off the pile when I'm interrupted.

"That's a lot of clothes you've got there," says a familiar voice. I look over to the other row of washers and swallow hard. In front of me is the guy that defended me in my COM class. His amber eyes sparkle as he looks at the mound of clothes that's thankfully covering my blushing face as I kneel behind the washer. After letting out a breath I didn't know I was holding, I push my hair back from my face, stand up, and put my hand on my hip.

"Well, I have a lot of clothes." *Yeah, he just said that.* "I mean I—I *own* a lot of—most of it is jeans and tops and—" He raises his eyebrows and tries not to laugh. "I just like to shop sometimes." My face gets redder at my inability to articulate, but the guy snorts as he looks down at his pile of clothes.

"You say that like it's a bad thing." He throws his shirts, jeans, and boxers into the wash then puts his palms on top of the machine and watches me sort through my things. Trying to cover for my earlier blunder, I clear my throat and think about what I want to say before I open my mouth.

"I, um... I wanted to say thanks for standing up for me today in COM134. I tried to catch you after class, but I couldn't find you." The boy raises his eyebrows in a sneaky way as I look up from my pile. His gaze gives me goosebumps. "Taylor was being a jerk, and he clearly doesn't take me seriously."

The boy scoffs. "He doesn't take anyone or anything seriously. I sit in front of him all the time. Sorry you were the one who got stuck sitting next to him today."

"It's alright. Makes me tougher," I joke, watching as a corner of the boy's mouth twists up into a partial smile.

"I don't know how he got into college, let alone Resslar," says the boy. I raise my eyebrows in shock as I laugh a little. "I'm serious! He's an asshole."

"Well, you're right about that." I take a deep breath as I throw the last of my things into the washer. "You know, I never did get your name."

"Oh, my bad. I'm Nate. Nate Stevenson."

"I'm Brooklyn Perce." Nate raises his eyebrows at my name.

"Like the city?" he asks, and I nod. "Wow, that's sick. How'd your parents come up with that?"

"That's where my parents met, and their obsession kind of got out of hand." He snorts, the little smile still on his face. My brain quickly flips through options of conversation starters and tells my mouth to move. "Do you live in this building?"

"No, I live over in Cypress, but I come here because all of the machines in Cypress are usually taken since there are only fifteen of them for about 300 kids," explains Nate.

"Makes sense," I say, unscrewing the cap on the bottle of detergent and pouring it into the washer.

"Plus, the girls in this building are cuter." At that, my hand jerks which makes the bottle of detergent move, so it spills onto the floor instead of into the spout. That's when Nate actually lets out some laughter. My face becomes red. "You good?" I calmly clear my throat, pour a little liquid into the machine, seal the bottle, and look at his gorgeous face. Nate shakes his head nonchalantly.

"Yeah. Fine," I say, clearing my throat, trying to recover. Nate shrugs and pushes the buttons on the washer to start it. I do the same as I avoid eye contact.

"I wasn't talking about you, by the way. Other girls."

"Right." Nate gives me a kind smile that makes his amber eyes shine. "Well, I've got a show to watch, but it was nice talking with you!" After he raises his right eyebrow slightly, I walk towards the door to leave and am about to go back into the hallway when–

"Brooklyn!" I turn around and lean on the doorframe, trying not to stare for too long at Nate. I mentally prepare for whatever romantic thing he's about to say. It'll be just like the movies: he'll say he wants to take me out, and I'll reply in that cute girlish way I can sometimes pull off. My heart almost stops as Nate opens his mouth.

"You forgot your laundry bag."

3

"And he's *gorgeous,* Kenni. He looks like he could easily be the fourth Hemsworth brother or something."

"No way," Kenni says. "He's seriously *that* good-looking?"

"Yeah!"

"How haven't I seen this guy before?"

"I'm still convinced I'm hallucinating him, to be honest," I admit. Drew sits down next to me with a sandwich and sighs.

"You're still talking about Nate?" groans my exasperated roommate. I slightly whine through my lips and put my head on the table as my hair splays out around me.

"Yes," I resign.

"You should've seen her when she came back up from the laundry room, Kenni," Drew says to my friend, shaking her head. "It was like a cartoon where the character's eyes turn into hearts." I look up from the table and give her a little glare. All she does is smile innocently.

"He lives in Cypress?" Kenni asks. I pick my head up and push my hair back into the curls I styled it into today.

"Yeah!" I say, still in a whiny tone.

"Ask Finn if he knows him," suggests Kenni.

"I doubt it," I tell her, looking at the ceiling as I think of another possibility. "But if Finn knew Nate before I met him and he didn't introduce us, I'm going to sue."

"How can you think about Nate when it's your first day at the radio station?" Drew asks as she bites her grilled cheese.

"I'M SO EXCITED!" I shout, snapping out of my daydream. I say it so loudly that half of the people who are sitting around us in the dining hall look at me, causing me to stare at my salad. "I'm so excited," I whisper again.

"And, with any luck, maybe this Ryker guy will be hotter than Nate," Drew says to Kenni, widening her eyes and smiling. Kenni grins and takes a swig of her coffee.

"Not possible. Not even *close* to being possible," I tell them. "No one is hotter than Nate."

"What about Zac Efron? He's pretty hot," Kenni quips before taking another sip.

"Even when he played Ted Bundy?" Drew questions, giving me a concerned gaze.

"Yeah!" When Drew and I say nothing and just stare with contained smiles at each other, Kenni gets up in a huff. "Are you judging me? You know what…"

"Dude, c'mon, you're gonna leave?" Drew says.

"I'm not gonna leave. I just want a cookie." Kenni walks away with her plate to the cookie cabinet near the seemingly endless row of cereal. I check my phone to look at the time. Thirty minutes. That's all. My leg is shaking under the table in anticipation.

"You cold or something?" Drew asks slowly, clearly noticing my shaking.

"What? Oh no! No, I'm just-I'm just excited about WRDW," I reassure her.

"I would be too. Hey, do you have time to help me tonight? My professor wants me to try to make a clay bust of someone. Fair warning, though: I can't promise that you will look remotely like yourself." I shrug.

"As sweet of an invitation as that is, I don't think I'm the right person to sculpt. I don't know how late I'm going to be at the station."

"Alright. I'll drag Finn out of his dorm."

"That'll be good." Drew smiles and pushes her blue-brown hair back from her eyes.

"It's gonna be miserable to sculpt his hair. It's so flowy," she gripes, suddenly becoming angry.

"But you love that, dontcha?" mutters Kenni, returning with a cookie for each of us.

"What was that?" snaps Drew.

"Hm what? Oh nothing!" Kenni winks at me with a sneaky smile. I take a cookie from her plate and nibble on it, returning her expression. Drew glowers at Kenni before swiping a cookie from her plate and eating it in four bites. As much as I try to eat the cookie slowly, my anticipation is building. I throw the rest of the cookie in my mouth, stand, and sling my backpack over my shoulder.

"I'll see you guys later!" I say excitedly through my mouthful of cookie. My friends shout their good-byes to me as I leave.

I practically run out of the dining hall, down the huge flight of stairs, and to the edge of campus by the Biology Building. Everyone I pass doesn't understand how happy I am as I run across the street without checking for cars or buses first. I could've died. I don't really care. The sun is shining, it's a great day. But when I go to turn the corner, my attention is pulled elsewhere.

Even though it's sunny out and there's not a cloud in the sky, there appears to be a gloomy haze over the white house with the red shutters on the corner. The windows on the first floor are boarded up and some on the upper levels are broken, smashed by rocks or bricks. There are four columns sitting on each of the corners of the porch off of the front of the house. On top of the white pillars sits a balcony that's accessed by the two white doors embedded into the siding. Distressed red shutters are hanging off of the trim around the windows, just one bad gust of wind away from crashing to the ground. The red front door is boarded up with two long planks of wood making a giant X under the Greek letters Sigma Eta Alpha that hang in proud, albeit faded, red metal letters above the doorway. The house doesn't look like it's been touched in more than a decade except for the short fenced-in lawn in front of it. It's terrifying, but I can't help but wonder why it's just sitting here vacant.

My feet unconsciously carry me past the crumbling black fence and to the foot of the front stairs of the haunted house. My eyes see the 'NO TRESPASSING' sign right outside of the door, but my brain chooses to ignore it. I want to run away, but something keeps me rooted there. Slowly, I go up the stairs, and my hand reaches out to the doorknob through a hole in the wooden X. I'm just about to try to open it—

"Excuse me!" I turn around and catch my breath. A campus police officer is looking at me from the sidewalk, his hands on his hips. "What are you doing?"

I go down the stairs and clear my throat. "Sorry Officer. I was just curious," I say.

"Maybe keep that curiosity in check next time. Didn't you see the sign?" asks the C.P. officer.

"I did. I'm sorry Officer, I won't do it again." The officer nods and snaps the gum he's chewing. Now that I'm closer to him, his height is somewhat intimidating. Maybe it's the fact that I can't see his eyes behind his dark aviator sunglasses, but his stare gives me the creeps. It makes me want to shrink down and crawl in a hole, never to be seen again.

"Don't stick your nose where it doesn't belong, alright? It could get you hurt."

I nod, understanding. "Have a good one, Officer." The officer watches me round the corner, his unseen eyes pushing me away.

✳ ✳ ✳

I take my ID and swipe in to the inconspicuous, small brick building a block off campus. When I open the door and look to my left, there's a reception desk and across the hallway is the room where I waited for my interview. There's no one in the waiting area besides a somewhat lanky boy on his phone. His height is given away by the way his legs seem to crumple on the ground. He wears a pair of worn jeans, old sneakers, and a maroon t-shirt underneath a green jacket. His thick brown hair is in a quiff style, but the sides of his head aren't too short. He has a little stubble on jaw, and he is biting his lip deep in thought as he looks as his phone. I fix my hair before I walk up to him.

"Excuse me," I say as sweetly as I can. The guy looks into my eyes, and I'm paralyzed for a second by how bright green they are. "I'm looking for Ryker Williams. Do you know where he is?"

The boy's face lights up in a smile. "Yeah I do. Let me show you where he is." The boy stands up, and I estimate his height to be a little over six feet. He takes me through an open doorway into a room with little recording booths off of it. The room is plain besides concert posters on the wall and little reporting souvenirs from years ago like press passes and admittance wristbands. The boy shows me to an editing booth and opens the door. The little room has a desk with a mixing board attached to a computer. There's no one in it. Confused, I turn around and look at the guy who is acting as though this is perfectly normal.

"Um," I say slowly. The boy perks up like he forgot something, then pushes past me and sits down in one of the two rolling chairs behind the desk. He looks at me and smiles a goofy, lopsided grin.

"Hi, I'm Ryker Williams. And you are?"

I let out a little laugh and offer my hand to shake his. "Brooklyn Perce."

Ryker looks at my hand and scoffs, that little smile still on his face. "Nice to meet you." He shakes my hand and then looks me up and down. I watch him look at my dress and then meet his eyes. "You normally look this... fancy?"

"Um..." I trail off, not actually sure what to say. I'm clearly overdressed, there's no doubt about it, but I have no excuse as to why.

Ryker winks at me. "Not that good with words, huh?" he teases.

"I am. I just don't have a good answer for you," I say truthfully.

Ryker smiles reassuringly. "Don't worry, you're good. All of us just look casual here. It's rare I even see a girl in a dress." Ryker gets out of the chair and motions for me to come with him. "So, today you're going to be given a tour and then trained. Don't worry, it's not as boring as it sounds, *and* you've been given the best mentor ever, so you'll survive." Ryker leads me out of the plain room and back into the hallway. We go up the stairs and down the hallway that houses Peter's office. Ryker stops at Peter's door, pokes his head in, and knocks. "Peter!" From what I can see, the office is still immaculately decorated with only slightly more papers on the large desk than there was before.

Peter turns around in his chair and gives me a smile when he sees me. "Brooklyn. So nice to see you," he says, although he sounds more tired than pleased to see me.

"You too," I say. Ryker turns to go, but Peter has another request.

"Ryker, when you show her around, makes sure she doesn't touch anything she doesn't know how to use."

Ryker gives his boss a thumbs up. "No problem." I wave goodbye to Peter and we continue to walk down the hallway. "Sorry about him. He's a good guy, it's just he doesn't like new people very much. Even when they have the experience you have, the equipment's expensive and he's got to be the one to replace it if it breaks."

"I understand," I say. "So, what am I mainly going to be reporting on?"

"Local news. We'll give you the recording of an interview one of us upperclassmen did earlier in the day or maybe the day before, you log tape or transcribe what they say, pull soundbites from the audio, then write the story. Pretty standard stuff that I'm sure you've done before."

I nod. "I did that all the time."

"Training you should be easy then. The other guy we had in here lasted about a week before he straight-up disappeared, hence your being here. He didn't know how to do anything, but you know what you're talking about, so don't disappear on us, yeah?"

"Promise I won't," I say as Ryker takes me into the main studio. There's one desk in the middle of the small room with the soundboard on it and a microphone coming off of the soundboard. Ryker waves hello to the girl sitting at the desk who waves back, then he motions for me to get out of the room. Once the door shuts, he starts talking again. "That was Syd. She has her own radio show, a sort of mash between music and talk show."

"Pretty cool," I comment.

"You'll mostly be doing news and stuff like that, so you'll probably never see her." Ryker opens another door next to the main broadcasting studio and my eyes are assaulted by tons of framed pictures on the walls of this mid-sized office. There must be forty on one wall. Boxes are stacked three high all around the office. There's one desk with an old Microsoft desktop on top of it hidden by boxes in the back-left corner.

"What the hell are these?" I ask.

"The station sponsors Greek life on campus. These are all the frats we support and since no one has the energy to take them off of the walls, there are pictures from the nineties. Super old stuff," Ryker explains.

"What's this room for?"

"I really have no idea, it's just a nice room to write your stories in because no one ever comes in here. I mean, it's nice if you don't mind all these people staring at you," jokes Ryker, taking a second to look around the room. When he looks at a plaque that's closer to him, he flinches like one of the kids is going to come alive and pop out at him. He composes himself as though nothing happened and clears his throat. "The tour continues, Ms. Perce." I roll my eyes at him and leave the frat room.

"So how long have you worked here?"

"Four years. I started as a freshman and worked my way up so now as a senior, I'm the student manager of the station. Maybe it'll happen to you one day," says Ryker, opening the door to another room for me.

"I hope so. I've wanted to work here ever since I was a kid," I tell him.

"I literally know *no one* who has wanted to work at a radio station since they were a kid," he says.

I laugh at that. "Honestly, me neither."

"Makes you *special*," Ryker says in mock awe. "You'll do well here. Don't worry."

I try not to.

4

When my tour ends and my training is over, Ryker gives me a WRDW lanyard with a generic-looking I.D. on it. "This is how you'll get in and out of the building since your R.U.I.D. could get lost or stolen. Just remember to bring the station I.D. every time you come," he says. I put the lanyard around my neck, but Ryker shakes his head. "Put it in your pocket. Around your neck makes you look like a freshman." I take it off and shove it in my pocket. Ryker nods approvingly. "There you go. See you later, Brooklyn." He says it with a small smile on his face. After my dismissal, I leave out of the front door and do my best not to skip all the way home. So *this* is what it feels like to have your dream job.

I stop carelessly walking when I get to the SHA house as the same funny gut feeling I got earlier passes over me again. I can't help but walk a couple feet towards it, even though the C.P. officer told me to stay away. If it's possible, the house gets creepier the longer I stare at it. My phone buzzes in my pocket which snaps me out of my daze. The Caller I.D. says 'Drew', so I pick it up and put it to my ear.

"Hello?"

"Guess what just happened?" I'm taken aback by how upbeat my roommate sounds.

"What?"

"I was just asked to photograph a concert downtown! They're gonna get me a pass and everything! Apparently, I have promise as a photographer!" She's talking so fast that I only understand part of her sentence.

"That's fantastic, Drew! When is it?"

"They said they'd get back to me with the details."

"Wow, that's awesome! I'm coming home now. You can tell me about it when I get back! I'll see you in a few." I hang up with my roommate and then start up the back stairs. The back stairs are a shorter but steeper set of stairs that you have to walk halfway down the hilly driveway of Smith to get to. If you need to get to the Biology Building or Frat Row which is near the radio station, that's the staircase to take. Halfway through the climb, I'm stopped.

"Well, well. Look who it is." Nate. He's looking down at me with a sneaky smile. "If I knew I was gonna see you, I would've dressed a little better." It's all I can do to not snort. He looks straight out of a Ralph Lauren catalog in a dark blue quarter zip, khaki shorts, and a white collared shirt.

"Where are you going?" I ask him.

"Where are you coming from?" he asks me.

I smile. "I asked you first," I say.

Nate rolls his eyes. "Smart girl. I'm going to visit my friend. He's in a frat, and I want to make a good impression on the other guys for rush next week. Now you."

"I'm coming from the radio station I work for," I say. Nate leans against the railing to let someone pass him as he crosses his arms.

"Oh, you work at a radio station? Which one?" he asks.

"WRDW," I say proudly. Nate lets out a low whistle.

"Hardly anyone gets on the staff as a freshman there. That's the word around Rosenburg anyway. You must be good." I grin at him and he raises an eyebrow. "You know, with a smile like that you should be on TV, not behind some speaker in a car."

"You're sweet," I say like a stupid ten-year old girl. He seems proud of himself that he made me simper.

Nate reaches in his pocket and pulls out his phone to check the time. "Shit, I have to go. But hey, what are you doing later?" My stomach flops over.

"What?" I ask like a dumbass.

"Do you have any plans for later?" he repeats.

"Nothing! No, nope, none." I mentally kick myself for saying the word 'no' about a million times. Nate hands me his phone.

"Put your number in. We'll get dinner in the dining hall or something. I need to get away from my friends." I gladly put my number in his phone and then hand it back to him. Nate grins again. "See you later, Brooklyn." After he goes down the stairs, I climb the rest of the steps and sink against the other side of the fence at the top to catch my breath. When I close my eyes, all I can see are his beautiful amber irises shining.

"Holy shit," I say as I breathe out. The brisk air doesn't do much to fight the heat in my face, but after I run the rest of the way up the hill, my nose has become numb.

I burst into my room and flop down on my bed. My station lanyard lies somewhere on the floor as I look at the ceiling dreamily. Drew looks over her laptop at me. I start to giggle, then laugh, then cry happy tears. Drew's eyes grow more concerned.

"You good?" she questions.

"Drew, I was just asked out by Nate. I'm *so* good," I tell her in between laughter. Drew's jaw drops as she slams her computer shut.

"No way!" she exclaims.

I nod and put my hands on my face. "This day is freaking amazing." I sigh.

I slide off of my bed like putty and just lie on the floor for what I think is an hour as I bask in the glory of my life at the moment.

❄ ❄ ❄

The next day, I go to class and keep my phone on vibrate in my pocket just waiting for a text from Nate. He said he'd see me later. I would rather 'later' be now. I go through my day mindlessly and find myself in the dining hall with my friends before I know it.

We're having a family dinner of sorts. Around six o'clock, Finn, Drew, Kenni and I are sitting around a table eating and chatting among all of the other friend groups. Family dinner only happens on rare occasions when our free time lines up but when it does, my friends make me laugh until my sides hurt. Finn sits down next to Drew across the table from me with two hot dogs and a cheeseburger on his blue plastic plate. Kenni snorts as she eats her salad.

"You know, I don't know how you manage to eat all of that and gain zero weight. If I tried to eat that much in one sitting, I would be the size of a house," Kenni says. Finn smiles with a mouthful of hot dog.

"It's because I work out," he brags through the bun in his mouth. I see Drew smile to herself.

"You're an engineering student, how do you have time to go to the gym?" Kenni asks. Fin holds up five fingers to indicate the time as he swallows. "You go at five *in the morning?*" she laughs.

"You liar," teases Drew, looking at me and rolling her eyes. The conversation enters a characteristic lull, but I pick it back up.

"Hey, have you guys been down near the Bio Building?" I ask.

"Yeah I have," says Kenni, "I have a class in there."

"Have you seen that creepy frat house on the corner?"

"What frat house?" Finn asks in a more serious tone.

"The one that's on the corner of the street down there," I say slowly. Finn nods.

"Oh yeah, I've seen that one." He puts down the burger he's eating and tries to act like he didn't just halt an entire conversation. My eyes narrow.

"What's wrong?"

"Nothing... it's just... I've been told my dad was in a frat." Drew, Kenni, and I exchange a look. Finn never talks about his real parents. He avoids the subject like the plague.

"Yeah? Do you know which one?" Drew says calmly, looking at our friend with care. Finn shakes his head and picks up his second hot dog.

"Nope. It's the only thing I know about them, other than the fact they didn't want me." He takes an aggressive bite from his burger, finishing it off as Kenni, Drew, and I share a look. "Screw my biological parents though," he says, taking a bite of his hot dog. He breathes in deeply and then exhales, swallowing the bun. He notices how quiet we three are and tries to lighten the mood. "Let's talk about something else, yeah? Drew, I heard you got a gig shooting a concert!" Drew perks right up and starts to excitedly talk about the performance. I'm still thinking about Finn's parents. How could an adoption agency hold information from a kid, especially a kid of his age? And why would his adopted parents tell him nothing about his biological parents besides the Greek life thing? Out of all the things to tell him, *that* one fact? My train of thought gets interrupted by Kenni.

"Earth to Brook! Hello?" she says, snapping her fingers in front of my face. I shake my head and look at her with a slight annoyance.

"I'm here! I'm good," I assure her.

"You were staring at Finn," Drew says with a touch of jealousy in her voice.

"Can't blame her," sighs Finn, "I *am* extremely attractive." Drew rolls her eyes and throws a piece of lettuce at him. He laughs, rips off a piece of the hamburger bun, and throws it back at her.

"You guys are children," Kenni scolds. Finn raises an eyebrow.

"No, I'm not. I enjoy the finer things in life." Finn shoves the last of his burger into his mouth. "Like dining hall cheeseburgers."

"Oh yeah, those are top tier," says Kenni. Finn and Drew both start arguing about burgers but before Kenni gets sucked into the conversation, I turn to her.

"Have you walked by that frat house?" I ask her. Kenni pops a carrot into her mouth and it makes an obnoxious crunching sound as it's crushed between her teeth.

"Yeah. It's so creepy, right? The house looks dilapidated as hell," says Kenni. She laughs to herself.

"What?" I ask.

"The first time I walked by it, I swore I saw a ghost or something pop out of a window," she says in a spooky tone. When she sees my somewhat freaked out expression, she laughs. "Oh c'mon Brook. I'm joking! You really think it's haunted or something?"

"I don't know. By the way the cop talked to me when I went up to it, it might be." I shrug. Finn stops his argument with Drew when I mention the police.

"A *cop*? Since when are you talking to cops?" Finn says.

"I didn't talk to him by choice! I walked up to the frat house and the cop just—"

"Whoa, whoa, whoa. You *stepped* on the creepy frat's *front lawn*? Well, you're possessed now," Finn jokes. Kenni and Drew laugh as I roll my eyes. "Seriously Brooklyn, if the cop told you to stay away from it, it's probably for the best."

"Probably," I echo.

5

"So, that's the end of the lecture today about the movie industry. Go see something this weekend, boost that box office revenue." My COM134 professor finishes up his sentence and looks at his watch. "You know, I don't want to launch into a new subject today. We'll get into TV next class. Have a good day." There's the sound of shuffling papers in binders and the sound of those binders closing as everyone packs up their things. I try to linger so I can get out at the same time as Nate. It's been a week since he's given me his number and no matter how many times I've checked my phone, a text from him refuses to pop up. Nate goes for the door, and I *conveniently* go for it at the same time. When we reach for the knob, he looks at me, smiles, and holds the door open as I go through. I can practically hear Taylor's eyes rolling as he walks out of class behind me. I see Nate go in the opposite direction of me and my heart sort of falls.

My feet take me to Newsworthy Cafe, the little eatery inside of the Rosenburg School of Communications. It's my main college within the university which means all of the classes pertaining to my major are in Rosenburg. I spend too much time in this building, but at the same time, it feels like home.

I find an empty table by the wall of windows, set my things down, and pull my laptop out of my bag. I get ready to do my food studies homework and put my headphones in, turning up my Spotify playlist. Once I've made up meals for the past week and put them into a food log, I edit my video for another multimedia communications class. I search for the right music on YouTube and clean up the crappy editing to get it ready for submission. I must've sat there for a while because the next time I look up from my Mac, the sky is getting dark and I am one of six people in the cafe. I pack my backpack, pull on my coat, and start to walk out of the building with my earbuds in.

"Brooklyn! Hey Brooklyn!" I don't hear my name the first time, but once I pull my right headphone out of my ear, I can clearly hear the voice of a familiar boy calling my name. I turn around and see Nate jogging to catch up with me.

"Hey!" I exclaim. Nate slows down and starts to walk with me. In the setting sunlight, his amber eyes glow like a wolf's. "Where are you coming from?"

"Work!" he says.

"Where's that?" I ask.

"At the Hold. I had to get to training after class today," he explains. *Ah, so that's why he couldn't talk to me.* The Hold is a library of sorts where students from Rosenburg can check out industry equipment to use to make their projects. It has video cameras, tripods, and lighting sets that each cost a semester's tuition. "I just started the other day. But enough about me. How have you been?"

"Um, I've been good! I started to work at the radio station last week, and I'm going there tomorrow for my first story," I tell him.

"That's so cool! I'm sorry I haven't been able to text you, by the way. I'm rushing a frat, and I don't really have time to do other stuff," Nate explains.

"Oh, it's no problem." I try to play it off as no big deal, but I think he can tell my slight annoyance.

"Are you, uh, gonna go to a movie this weekend? Take our professor's advice?" he teases.

"Sadly no, I need to binge *The Office* for the third time."

"I love that show," Nate says. "Favorite character is…?"

"Dwight," we both say at the same time. We laugh at each other and pass more students on our way back home.

"I just watched *Brooklyn 99* for the first time, so I watch *The Office* in between each binge to cleanse myself," I tell him.

"My brothers love *Brooklyn 99*, but I could never get into it. Makes sense for you though, your name is in the title."

"You should try it again! It takes a few episodes to get used to Andy Sandberg," I admit. Nate shakes his head, smiling.

"Yeah, maybe I will." He pauses. "Tell you what. I feel like shit for blowing you off this week. Do you want to come to a bid event with me? As a friend." I look at him with a raised eyebrow. Nate laughs. "I should explain. So, this entire week has been rush and now since I got a bid, there's this formal thing where I have to bring a date. After that, I can decide whether or not to become a pledge."

"Shouldn't your date be in a sorority? Or even be *interested* in rushing a sorority?" I ask.

"Eh, it's suggested, but all the guys in the frat know me, so I'm practically in anyway. Plus, I'm not opposed to breaking the rules a little if you aren't." Nate gives me this side smile that makes me internally melt.

"Of course I'm not. But if I'm your date, won't the guys think we're together?" I test.

"Eh…" Nate trails off. We laugh a little together and get to the top of the stairs. A few of Nate's friends pass and give him high fives. I see Finn walking down the path in gym clothes and my face lights up.

"Hey Finn!" I say. Finn stops and gives me a smile.

"Hey Brook! Who's, uh, who's your friend?" Finn asks with a sneaky smile towards me. Nate pulls his hand out of his pocket and offers it to Finn who takes it.

"Nate Stevenson," says Nate. Finn shakes his hand.

"Finn Larson." They nod hello once they drop their handshake. Finn looks down the path that leads to the stairs as though he's still checking if it exists.

"What day is it today?" I ask him.

"Leg day, Brook. I need to get back up those damn stairs afterwards. Pray for me."

I nod and put my hands together like I'm calling on God. "I will," I promise.

Finn claps me on the shoulder. "My quads thank you. I'll see you later, Brook! Nice meeting you, Nate!"

"Likewise," Nate says, giving Finn a wave as he keeps walking. The two of us keep walking towards the dorm but I turn around to look at Finn who's walking backwards giving me two thumbs up. I snort to myself.

"So, who's he?" Nate asks when I turn back around.

"Oh, Finn? Finn's my friend," I say. "He knows everyone." Nate laughs.

"I have a few buddies like that. I don't know how they remember everyone's names," he says. We stop at the front steps of Smith, and I turn around to look at him. Nate looks back towards his dorm and then looks slightly down at me like he's thinking. "Hey, do you want to get some food? I'm starving."

"Sure!" I say enthusiastically. As we walk towards the dining hall, I feel my hand hold onto his.

The dining hall is packed since it's peak dinnertime. Once we swipe our I.D.s and grab a plastic plate, we wander around the dining hall, seeing what there is to eat. I settle on a salad and a few pieces of seasoned grilled chicken. Meanwhile, Nate has piled onto his plate a massive salad with shredded chicken, croutons, a boiled egg, cut tomatoes, cucumbers, shredded carrots, and more. We get a booth in the corner of the dining hall and sit across from each other. Nate picks up a fork and starts to dig in as I cut my chicken.

"So, Brooklyn Perce, tell me about your life. Beginning to end," says Nate with a little smile.

"Um, from start to finish?" I say.

Nate chuckles. "From start to finish" he echoes.

"Alright." I take a sip of water before starting. "My childhood wasn't that exciting. I did tap dancing and quit, did soccer then quit, played the violin then quit. The only thing I kept consistent was writing. I loved to write. I used to make these little picture books and read them to my stuffed animals. They were an easily amused audience." Nate smiles at the thought of me reading to my teddy bear. "I used to 'report' on things, too."

"Like solving things?"

"Yeah, sort of. Like this one time, my neighbor Mike got his Razor scooter stolen. I did some digging—and by 'digging' I mean I asked around— and it was his brother." Nate snorts in amusement since his mouth is full of salad. "Then, my friend Marcy lost her cat, and after doing 'research', I found him two days later underneath my deck. Every time I solved something, I wrote it in this little diary. I actually found it when I was cleaning out my room last time and reading back through it was pretty funny. I thought I was so special just because I found some poor girl's cat."

"Hey, I'm sure she was thankful."

"She was! And it was kind of fun to play investigative reporter. I liked the puzzle of it...I really liked doing actual puzzles too, so that's probably where that came from." I sigh. "Then my parents split when I was about eleven. They had been fighting for a while. I was really sad about it, but when I got older, my mom told me my father was being a jerk and the relationship was starting to go downhill. She said they broke up to do what was best for me." I laugh to myself as Nate's smile slips away.

"God, I'm sorry. That's horrible." He sounds genuinely sad for me. I wave it off.

"It's alright. I mainly live with my mom in New Jersey about an hour south of here and we have the sweetest dog, Harley. I miss him so much," I say wistfully, thinking of my best friend.

"What kind of dog?" he asks.

"A Bernese." Nate's eyes widen.

"Damn, they're huge. Where does your dad live?" Nate asks.

"He works at a real estate firm in Philadelphia, so he moved to an apartment there after he and my mom split. Anyway, I have no siblings, so I get a car to myself which is nice," I joke. I take a few more bites of chicken. "And I'm a broadcast journalism major as you know. My dream is to be a radio personality."

"I've never met anyone whose dream is to be on the radio," Nate says thoughtfully.

"That's what my boss at the station said. I guess most people haven't," I tell him.

"Are you happy you came here?"

"Hell yeah. I've wanted to go to Resslar since I was little. Living close to here, I always came up for basketball games and stuff. It's always been my home-away-from-home, so while I miss being at my *actual* home, this is still amazing." I relax back into my seat. "Now, tell me about you! Everything!"

"Alright, well you should know I'm the youngest of three. All boys," he clarifies when I raise my eyebrows.

I sigh. "Wow, that's insane. Your poor parents," I say. Nate snorts.

"We weren't that bad. I sort of had the little sibling complex though. My brothers were way better than me at virtually everything, especially sports. My oldest brother, Colin, is just out of college and is working in New York City. He lives with his girlfriend. He played baseball in college. My other brother, Derek, is a senior at Duke and plays lacrosse. He's been on the team since he was a freshman. He was actually recruited in his second year of high school," Nate tells me.

"He's that good?" I ask with wide eyes. Nate nods with his mouth full.

"Oh yeah, my brothers are talented. Which left me with little to work with," he says.

I scoff. "Oh c'mon, you're talented!"

"Yeah? How so?" I look him up and down and then smile at my plate.

"You stick up for me…and you're kind and pretty handsome," I say in a little voice. Nate runs a hand through his hair.

"Aw, don't flatter me, Perce," he says sheepishly. He gives me a wink. "But thank you."

I smile, my face turning pink as I pick at the food in front of me. "More!" I prompt him.

"Alright, where was I? Right, my talented brothers! So, I gave up on trying to athletically out do my brothers in high school. I played football for a few seasons, I dabbled in lacrosse for a while, and I guess I did well. I played okay, but not like them. It also didn't help that whenever I screwed up, my coach would be like, 'Your brother would never!' So, I turned to journalism. I learned I could write and just kind of went from there."

"Did you like any of your brothers?" Nate looks at the ceiling in thought. "When they weren't kicking your ass at everything." He laughs at me and looks back down at his salad.

"Yeah, they were fine when they were around. We would make forts in the woods behind our house and play with our Irish setter Marlin who died when I was about nine. Colin and I were really into Legos, though."

"Who wasn't?" I comment.

48

"Right? One time, my brothers and I built a Lego tower with my dad that reached the ceiling. He had us up on his shoulders when it got too tall." He smiles fondly. "Sometimes I miss being with them. They live close by, though. I just visited Colin in the city last weekend before rush started."

"How'd you get into journalism?" I ask, taking a bite of food that's starting to become cold.

"I did newspaper in high school and, like you, I liked figuring out stories. We did this whole exposé on a teacher who stole from the field trip fund and that was, like, the best thing I've written. I loved working with that team. We had three people: Me, who wrote most of it, this girl named Liz, who did interviews and all that, and this guy named Jacob, who sort of went undercover."

"No way!" I say in between laughter.

"Yeah! It was great. He pretended to want his check back 'cause his mom needed it' and when the teacher couldn't give it back to him, we knew it was a story."

"Had he not gone on the field trip yet?"

"No, and we never did!" We chuckle a bit until Nate gets back on track. "It was really the people who made that class. I don't know if you can tell, but I love talking and I love people, so being a reporter is a natural choice."

"Sounds like a good fit," I say with a little smile. There's silence for a bit and then Nate asks me another question.

"What do you do here? Besides your radio station?"

"Nothing really. I try writing short stories from time to time but that's about it," I say casually. Nate puts his fork down in shock.

"You write short stories? That's so cool. Can I read one?"

"They're horrible."

"Bullshit, they can't be *that* horrible," Nate pries.

"Nate, hon, they're bad. They're not even finished! I get a page or two in and then stop. I've never finished one."

"Interesting. Well, can I read something you *are* proud of?"

"You can read my first WRDW story."

"I meant *fiction*, Brook."

I dramatically sigh. "Fine, you can read a few pages."

"Okay. Good compromise," he says, eating more of his food.

"Any hidden talents for you?" I ask, taking a sip of water.

Nate smiles and looks down at his plate. "Oh God," he mutters. Nate puts a hand behind his neck and rubs it.

"What?"

"It's, um, I can... I—uh." Nate can't seem to finish his sentence.

"C'mon Nate, what is it?" I prompt. Nate takes a deep breath in through his teeth and looks up at me.

"Okay, you know how I'm rushing a frat?" he starts. I nod. "Alright, well we had this Irish-themed event thing and some of the guys were mockingly step dancing to the music because they thought it was funny." My mouth drops open as he trails off. Nate laughs at himself. "And it pained me to watch because I actually took Irish Step Dance class." I almost burst out laughing but manage to keep it to a giggle for his sake. Nate leans back in the booth and looks at the ceiling melodramatically. "You think that's dumb."

"No, no that's amazing!" I reassure him, biting my lip to keep from laughing.

Nate narrows his eyes. "You're laughing at me."

I shake my head. "No, I'm not! I'm not laughing!" I put my hand over my mouth and look at him as he tries not to laugh too.

"I did it when I played football. It helped with the footwork!" Nate defends. "Plus, it was surprisingly fun!"

"Can you do it?"

Nate's eyebrows travel up higher on his forehead. "Do *what*?"

"Irish stepdance." Nate looks around like he's being watched.

"What, *here*?"

"Yeah *here*! C'mon, I'm letting you read my short stories—"

"Your *half-finished* short stories," Nate points out.

"Still!" Nate looks like he wished he'd never mentioned his talent. He stares at me and my wide smile.

"Share your stories with me." I whip out my phone, go to my Google Drive and pick my most recent work. I text him the link and sure enough, it *ping*s onto his phone screen. I put down my phone and look at him like an expectant puppy. Nate hangs his head slightly like he wasn't expecting me to be able to do that on the spot. Finally, after a minute of silence, he sighs.

"You can't film it," he says. I put my hands up in surrender so he can see they're nowhere near my phone. Nate slowly stands, clears his throat, and, looking straight ahead, hops up and down in the traditional fashion. I contain my laughter and just start clapping. Nate whisks his hair out of his face and sits back down, his cheeks flushed.

"Wow! Amazing," I compliment. "Do it again!"

"Not in a million years, Brook." Although he looks embarrassed, the smile on his face is larger than mine.

✹ ✹ ✹

I float into my building after hugging Nate goodbye. He kissed me on the cheek before he left, and he didn't want to let go of my hand. I feel like a pile of Silly Putty as I walk down the hallway in my building. When I collapse on my bed in my room, Drew takes out an earbud and looks at me.

"God, that kid has gotten to you," she snorts.

"How did you know it was Nate?" I ask her.

Drew shrugs. "Roommate instincts."

"He met Finn," I tell her, turning around and leaning against my bed, so I can talk to her.

Drew snaps to attention at the mention of Finn. "Oh God, what did Finn do?" she asks.

"He shook Nate's hand and did that chin nod thing. Finn was on his way to the gym, so he didn't say much but he gave me two thumbs up behind Nate's back, so I assume he approves," I say quickly. Drew blinks a few times.

"Okay you're gonna have to slow down and say that one more time," she laughs. I take a deep breath and explain it to her. I finish with details about the dinner and the invite to Nate's frat party. Drew wiggles her eyebrows at me.

"Oh, a *frat* thing? Brooklyn's gonna be the arm candy of a *frat* boy," Drew teases.

I roll my eyes and empty my bag onto my desk. "He said I'm going as a friend!" I tell her, sorting through my things and grabbing my phone.

"First it's as a friend, then it's gonna be as a date, then it's gonna be as his wife," Drew lists like it's inevitable.

"Alright, sure, I'll tell you when he proposes on the third date," I sarcastically promise.

"Ah-HA so you *admit* it's a date!" Drew exclaims, pointing at me in a final way. All of a sudden, I get a call from Ryker. I hit the little green button on my screen and put the phone to my ear. "Hello?"

"Ms. Perce?" Ryker says in a fake British accent. I snort to myself.

"Yes?" I say.

"Peter would like it if you would come to the station quickly and help write a last-minute story," continues Ryker in the stupid accent.

"Peter, huh?" I say, raising an eyebrow skeptically as I detect a bit of bullshit.

"Yes ma'am, Peter," he repeats.

"Drop the accent, Ryker. You sound crazy," I tell him.

"I thought it was good!" he says in his normal voice.

"No, it's not," I hear a faint voice say in the background.

"Oh, shove it, Lukas," he says, and I snort to myself. "Anyway, can you come? You can meet my asshole of a friend over here."

"If anyone's an asshole, it's you!" Lukas distantly defends.

"Alright, don't fight, I'll be there soon," I say.

"Thanks Brook!" Ryker hangs up and I roll off of my bed, pulling my jacket back on.

"Where the hell are you going?" Drew asks.

"They need me at WRDW. Some last-minute story they want me to work on." Drew nods in understanding. I grab my wallet and phone. "See you later."

I walk down the back stairs and start towards the radio station. With music in my ears, I cross the street by the Biology Building, so I pass the side of the creepy frat house. I look around to make sure there aren't any C.P. officers and then slowly approach the house. The closer I get to it, the more I want to run away from it. I thought it was ominous during the day, but I hadn't seen it at night. *If it looks this bad from the outside, I wonder what it's like on the inside.*

Fallen leaves crunch beneath my feet as I creep up to a window on the first floor. I hear something fall behind me. My head whips around to check behind my shoulder but no one's coming. It must've been an acorn from a tree or something. I cup my hands around my eyes to eliminate the glare from a streetlight and then look inside a musty window. I can't see much, but when I turn my phone flashlight on with one hand, I can somewhat see inside.

The inside of the house has floorboards that are ripped out, curtains that are torn down, beer cans in the corner, and some graffiti on the walls. Part of the ceiling's been chewed through by an animal and there are parts where the drywall has just fallen off and is now on the floor in a dusty heap. No one's touched this room since the house was abandoned which makes it even more terrifying somehow.

I quickly back away from the SHA house and continue my walk to the station. Every few feet I check behind me to make sure someone's not following me, but each time I check there's no one there. Once I get to the station, I turn around one more time and jump a bit as I hear the wind rustle a bush. *Pull it together, Brooklyn.* I swipe my card and quickly enter the station.

"Ryker?" I call out.

"In here!" I go towards his voice and see Ryker sitting there with the boy I assume is Lukas. With mousey brown hair, wire-rimmed glasses, and frumpy sweats, Lukas looks like he just rolled out of bed despite it being 7:30 at night. He doesn't look up at me as I come into the room.

"Hey, I'm Brooklyn," I say to him.

"Hi, I'm Lukas, and I'm sorry you have to work with Ryker," he says, not taking his eyes off of his laptop. Ryker, whose feet were crossed up on the desk, takes his work boots off of the table and sips from a coffee cup emblazoned with The Coffee Bean logo.

"You need to ingest caffeine. You suck when you're tired." Ryker forces Lukas to take the cup from him which Lukas takes then puts down on the table, going back to what he was writing. "Okay, maybe you just suck in general," Ryker mutters, getting to his feet. He smiles at me. "Thanks for coming in late. Could you just write a quick 200-word story about this audio clip we got today? The girl who was supposed to do it didn't get around to it, and we need it for the 8 o'clock news."

"Of course, just give me a computer," I tell him, happy that I've been trusted with such a close deadline. Ryker opens the door to an editing room right next to where Lukas is typing away. He pulls up the audio file on the computer for me and lets me get to work. As the interview starts coming out of the speakers, I open up a Word document and begin to transcribe it. I leave the door open so I can hear what Ryker and Lukas are talking about, but their conversation gets drowned out by my own thoughts.

What the hell happened to the inside of that house? Better yet, how many years does it take for a house to look like that and no one thinks to take it down? And what happened to the guys who lived there, whose house fell into such disrepair? I become so engrossed in mental questions that I don't realize the interview audio has long since ended. I snap myself back to reality and start the audio track over, this time listening to every word.

"So, dude, you going to that concert on Saturday?" I hear Ryker ask from outside.

"You'll have to be more specific, Williams," says Lukas.

"C'mon, your social calendar is *that* filled up that you need me to specify which concert?" Ryker groans.

"We live in a city, Ryker. There are concerts happening everywhere," says Lukas in his condescending tone.

"It's the one downtown with Young Yesterday headlining," Ryker angrily specifies.

"The one that Syd is going to?" Lukas asks.

"Yeah. I'm extending the invitation 'cause I know you wanna hook up with her." I hear Lukas throw something at Ryker. He dodges it and it lands on the desk behind him.

"I don't," he says.

"You'd be perfect for each other. You're both uptight," Ryker reasons.

"I despise you," Lukas says wistfully. I snort into the keyboard at that one. "Something funny back there?"

"No, no it's nothing. My roommate is photographing that concert though," I tell them, turning around in my swivel chair.

"Yeah? What's her name?" Ryker asks.

"Drew Samuels," I tell him.

"Can we use some of her pictures for online content?" he asks.

"I'm sure you can if you credited her. Let me text her." As soon as I fire off a text to Drew, I get one from Nate.

Heya Brook-Formal's on Saturday at 10.
Pick you up at five of 10 and we'll walk.
Formal so wear a dress...IDK I'll let you decide.

I quickly type a thumbs up Emoji before going back to writing the story. Drew answers me enthusiastically, so I roll my chair over to the door.

"Ryker, Drew says you can use some of her pictures. I'll send them to you when she gets them," I tell him.

"Sounds good. Tell her she's amazing," he responds. Ryker gets out of his chair and stands in the doorway of the editing suite I'm in as soon as I end my first draft.

"Damn, you work fast," Ryker says in admiration.

"Eh it's just a first draft. I have to rework the lead a little bit and find a coherent way to end it," I tell him.

"Be careful, Williams. She's gonna take your job," Lukas jabs.

"You shut up," says Ryker, pointing a finger at Lukas. He looks at me skeptically. "You seem off, Brooklyn. What's wrong with you?"

"Yeah Williams, *that's* the way to charm a girl. Ask her what's wrong with her," Lukas sighs.

"What did I *just* tell you about shutting up?" Ryker asks angrily. I snort as I go through my story.

"Nothing's wrong with me. I just have a lot on my mind," I say truthfully.

"Like what?" he pleads like a child. I'm reluctant to answer him. "C'mon Brooklyn, the three of us are the only people here."

"And Ryker loves knowing other people's business," Lukas deadpans. I sigh and look at his hopeful face.

"Well, I'm apparently going to a frat formal thing on Saturday," I tell him. Ryker bursts out laughing. "What?"

"You're in a sorority? Jesus, I was *so* wrong about you!" Ryker says in between laughter.

"Don't be a dick, Williams. A girl in a sorority is still a girl," chides Lukas.

"Oh, I'm not saying being in a sorority is bad. I've had my fair share of sorority girls," Ryker says. He crosses his arms and leans with his shoulder on the doorframe. "Just didn't think our little Brooklyn would be interested in a sorority."

"I'm someone's date to a fraternity event. I'm just helping him get in," I clarify. Ryker raises an eyebrow.

"Oh, so Brooklyn's got a boyfriend?" he says sneakily.

"You know, you're really hindering my ability to work," I tell him. Ryker puts his hands up in mock surrender.

"Well, I'm sorry if your supervisor wants to know more about you," he says. Ryker walks back out to Lukas who's still typing on his computer. Ryker starts to pick off bits of an eraser and beings to throw them into the hood on Lukas's sweatshirt. I try to refrain from snorting since Lukas just keeps on typing, not noticing the bits of pink rubber flying by his face.

I finish up my story within the next fifteen minutes and then call Ryker in for approval. The senior groans like I'm making him do an arduous task and then gets up to see what I've written. When he scans over the piece, his face turns from annoyed to surprised.

"Jesus, you can write," he mutters in between mouthing to himself the words I've written.

"Thanks," I say proudly.

"Yeah, this looks good. Email this to Lukas, and he'll give it a final edit before it airs." Ryker gets up and goes back to throwing eraser shavings into Lukas's hood. I quickly email it to Lukas whose address is on the wall of the editing room. When I get out of the editing suite, I lean against the door jamb like Ryker was doing before. He raises his eyebrows at me.

"Why are you still here? You can go," my boss tells me.

"I was just wondering if you could drive me back," I say. Ryker looks at Lukas who keeps his eyes glued to his computer.

"You know, I wish I could but I gotta keep throwing erasers into Lukas's hood," says Ryker. When that doesn't faze Lukas, Ryker tries a different approach. "Wish I could drive you home, Brook, but tonight's the night that I'm really gonna try to kill Lukas–"

"Drive the girl home, Williams," Lukas demands. Ryker smiles and claps Lukas on the back as he goes to the door.

"Atta boy. C'mon Brook, let's take you home."

I go outside and get into Ryker's beat-up black Saturn. Inside, the cloth seats are worn down and stained. The back seat has clothing, fast food bags, and other pieces of trash thrown carelessly onto the seat. The entire car has a distinct odor that I identify as weed mixed with some sort of air freshener that hasn't done its job. I make a note to only let Ryker drive me short distances.

"She's a bit old but she gets me around," says Ryker, clearly noticing how I look around at the interior. I buckle up as he shoves the key into the ignition and tries to turn the car over. The engine struggles to come to life, but its sputter finally turns into a purr. The Saturn rolls out of the WRDW driveway and onto the street, only to immediately stop for the light.

"I live in Smith," I tell him. Ryker nods.

"Gotcha. You must have some good leg muscles to get up those stairs every day," he jokes.

"Yeah, I do. Best calves on campus." Ryker laughs to himself. Then there's a pause before I talk.

"Hey, that weird frat house on the corner... How long has it been there?" I ask casually.

"The SHA one?" Ryker shrugs. "For as long as I can remember. I live around here, and it's always been there. It's shut down now. Something about hazing, I think." I nod, not wanting to say anything else. "What, you want to research it?"

"Maybe. It's worth a Google, at least. I keep thinking about the damn thing," I admit. Ryker shrugs.

"I don't know why you bother. It's not really worth looking into, honestly. Some of my buddies tried to break in there to smoke, and C.P. caught them before they got up the steps. It's gonna be there forever, no one cares enough about it to do anything."

There's another pause. "What frat is your boyfriend in?"

"He's not my boyfriend." I sigh.

"Yeah, but if I say boy-space-friend, it still sounds like I'm saying 'boyfriend', so he's your boyfriend," Ryker explains.

I smile to myself. "Clever. And I don't know, he hasn't officially declared yet."

"Formals are fun. The sorority ones are, anyway. Can't speak for the guys, but they're probably a good time. Just watch yourself."

"Thanks Dad," I joke. Ryker smiles.

"No worries." He pulls into the circle in front of my building. I say goodbye and thank him for the ride before slamming the door and going up the five stairs to get to my building. I get into my room and creep around to get ready for bed so as not to wake up Drew.

I keep thinking about the frat house that I passed. It's just so obviously creepy that there must be something wrong with it. Scoffing at myself, I shake it off. Ryker seemed to not give it a second thought, so why should I?

I shut the door quietly after returning from the bathroom and get ready for bed. I'm just about to put my phone away when I get a call. The Caller I.D. says *Unknown*. I let it go to voicemail, but the person calls again. Annoyed, I pick it up.

"Hello?" I snap.

"Stay away from the house, Brooklyn." The voice sends chills down my spine.

"Who is this?" I ask.

"Stay away from the house." The line goes dead, and I'm left listening to static.

6

And that's why you don't mess around with a fish," finishes Finn the next day at Friday night dinner. Kenni is staring blankly at Finn with a piece of lettuce hanging out of her mouth. After she snaps out of her shock, Drew finally lets out a nervous laugh that sounds more like the bleat of a goat.

"Well that's... that's a hell of a story Finn," Drew says. "Brook, what are— what are your thoughts on that?" She looks at me as I poke around my plate with a fork. When she sees I'm not listening, she hits me on the top of my head with her palm. I look up at her.

"Geez! What was that for?" I exclaim.

"I just told my fish story!" Finn says.

"And I'm sure it was thrilling. Now can I eat my food in peace?" I say in a snide tone. Kenni looks at Drew with her eyebrows raised.

"What's going on there, Brook?" Kenni says slowly. "Are you feeling okay?"

"Yeah. Yeah, I'm fine." Finn looks over at me.

"You're not fine. You seem super stressed," he says as he sips his water. "What's wrong?"

"I said nothing," I shrug. Kenni narrows her eyes.

"Alright. Doesn't mean there's not something wrong though."

"This'll make her feel better," says Drew to my friends as if I can't hear. "Brook, how's Nate?"

"He's good. I'm going to a frat thing for him tomorrow night," I say casually. Finn almost spits out his water. He swallows before asking me a question.

"Why the hell would you *willingly* go to a frat thing?" he questions. Before I can answer, he looks like he's figured something out and his mouth drops in shock. "Come *on* Brooklyn. Don't use him like that."

"Use who like what?" says Kenni, totally out of it. Finn scoffs and looks at me. I look down at my food to hide my aggravated expression from Kenni and Drew.

"She's gonna use Nate to get access to the frat world or whatever so she can figure out what the hell's going on with the house on the corner," he explains.

"That's not it at all," I finally snap, glaring at him. "Is it so difficult to believe that I actually *like* this kid?"

"No, but you can't tell me that the frat thing doesn't play a part in it," Finn argues.

"Why do you hate frats so much, Finn? I get your real parents were in one, but that doesn't mean they're *all* bad," I defend. Drew and Kenni are quietly watching us go back and forth like a tennis match over the table.

Finn sighs. "I know, I know they're not all bad. I just don't like them in general."

"Okay, so give Nate a chance. He's not a bad guy, I doubt his frat is bad either," I say in a final tone, finishing the spat. It's quiet at the table for a moment as all of us calm down, but of course Finn has to open his mouth again.

"I just… I thought your fascination with that frat house was gone, Brook. Why are you still looking into it?" he says.

"Because I think there's something wrong with it, okay?" I finally snap. Drew narrows her eyes.

"Something wrong with it? Like what?" she asks.

"I don't know. Something just doesn't sit right whenever I see it or think about it," I say.

"You know, I hear there's this thing called the Internet where you can look up *anything* about literally *everything*. Maybe look at that so you can get over this weird fascination," Finn suggests condescendingly. I glare at him and let the conversation drop as my friends share glances, wondering what insane idea I have inside of my head.

✳ ✳ ✳

Later that afternoon, I open a Google search tab and take a deep breath, closing my eyes. After letting out a huge puff of air, I type 'SHA fraternity Resslar University'. I get hundreds of results from news agencies throughout the northeast. I read one, then another, then another, then ten more. I click around on websites for about an hour, taking notes on a legal pad sitting on the desk beside me. My hand flies across the paper as I eagerly click around online, learning as much about the house as I can.

After I decide my eyes can't handle looking at the screen for another second, I shut my laptop in a final way and put my head in my hands. The notes I've taken look like chicken scratch, but I can tell what they say.

SHA Fraternity
Social all-male fraternity
Good reputation among business world

Unraveling

History at RU

Came to Resslar in 1950, shut down in 1997

Started off as serious, but then morphed into a frat that went through the motions instead of caring, only in it to have fun

Written up due to intense hazing before

Hazing lead to death of a brother in 1997

Causes of death: head trauma, possible strangulation (marks on neck)

Found outside of house

Parents wanted son to stay anonymous, didn't want a martyr or media storm

CP records say an emotionally unstable female student (girlfriend?) killed him

The news sites all say the same thing, just in different words. After quitting Google for the night, I'm left feeling even more curious than when I started. From what I've seen, the predominant theory is the brother's girlfriend killed him, but of course there's a ton of speculation. Some members within the community say Satan was involved, that the frat was cursed from the start. The Resslar University Society for Inexplicable Occurrences said aliens hijacked fraternity rush that year and had it out for the frat. I dismissed that theory the second I read it. The weirdest thing though is that none of the officers or school officials involved in the case seemed invested in the whole thing. It sends a chill up my spine to know that a student was murdered and no one seemed to care.

Drew slams her laptop shut from across the room which makes me jump, jolting me out of my intense train of thought. She turns around with a confused look.

"You good?" she asks.

"Yeah I'm fine." Drew jumps up onto her bed and starts to read a book about the elements of photography. I just lean back in my desk chair and stare at the notes I've written. Something gnaws at the inside of my stomach. I decide I need to find the C.P. reports from the night they found the body of the brother. Maybe the local police have something on it that I could access.

I open my laptop back up and search for the frat again, but this time I add the word 'reporting' onto the end of my query. A whole host of articles, local and national, come up and the headlines are less than favorable. I swallow hard as I read an article about a journalist from the school paper who was sent to the frat house to investigate. The guy went missing for two days then was found dead on the front lawn of the house, beaten like the victim. That in turn opened up a separate investigation, but nothing came of it. Authorities couldn't pinpoint an exact person or persons who killed the journalist. There's another story about a reporter from the city newspaper trying to reach out to members of the fraternity, but none of them would go on record. Only one anonymous source who was identified as 'a former Sigma Eta Alpha brother' had a direct quote in the article.

Says one brother, "The death of a brother is crushing. I've heard so many stories at this point, it's insane. I try to stay away from it, though, 'cause all I know is, you talk about it, you go missing."

The gnawing inside me consumes my entire body.

Saturday night, I try to remain calm as I look in the mirror and smooth the front of my dress. The bodycon cut shows every curve I have but thankfully it's somewhat ruffled so the fabric isn't flat. The deep scoop neckline with little gem detailing around it does me so many favors. When Drew looks me over, she whistles, impressed.

"You look good," she says honestly. "But there's something missing." She goes over to my closet and, in classic Drew fashion, pulls out my black leather jacket. "Put this on." With a sigh, I pull it on and then look at myself.

"Good call," I tell her.

"Well you aren't gonna wear that crappy rain jacket you wear everywhere. When is he coming?" she asks. I check my phone and see the time is five to ten.

"He should be here any minute," I say. My heart is going too fast. I haven't had anything to eat in fear of throwing it up since my stomach can't stop flipping over. I keep pacing around our room and checking my reflection to make sure my dark red lipstick isn't smudged and my winged eyeliner is still even. Drew hops onto her bed.

"Stop worrying. You'll be fine. And if you need me, just call," she reminds me. "I'll be at the concert, but I'll sprint over to that frat house ASAP."

"You're awesome," I tell her with a smile.

"I know," says my roommate with a wink. She looks around and then her eyes settle on her closet. "Let's get ready for the concert." She pulls out her red leather jacket, black ripped skinny jeans, and black tank top. "Perfect."

Knock-knock.

"Brooklyn? It's Nate!" calls my date from outside the door. I turn to Drew, suddenly becoming paralyzed.

"Open the freaking door, Perce!" Drew hisses excitedly. I slowly walk across the room, throw my curled hair over my shoulder, take a deep breath, then open the door.

Nate is wearing dark pants with dress shoes. On top, he has on a blue collared shirt with a black tie and jacket to match my dress. His dark hair is slightly gelled, so it keeps that side swoop it has. When he sees me, his amber eyes light up.

"Wow. You look beautiful," he says with a breath of air.

"You don't look too bad yourself," I compliment. I turn around to my roommate and wave good-bye. Nate and I walk down the hallway, and I hit the button to call the elevator. We step inside and take it all the way down to the first floor.

As we walk through the lobby, I feel every eye on us. I walk tall with my shoulders rolled back, proudly holding Nate's hand as we draw everyone's attention away from their work. Nate holds the door open for me as we exit the building into the crisp night air. The slight wind makes it a tad colder, but I don't feel it as I walk beside Nate and laugh at the story he's telling me about his rush experience so far.

"How many guys are in a pledge class per semester?" I ask him. Nate takes a second to think.

"Probably about 20 to 30. They're all great guys, but some of 'em are elitist. They think it's their right to be in whatever frat just because their dad or grandfather was in it," Nate tells me.

"So how do you beat them all out?" Nate lets out a bark of laughter.

"It's cheesy, but you honestly have to be yourself. It's way less intense than the sororities. You really just have to bond with the guys."

"What other frats have you visited?" He looks up to the sky as he tries to remember. "Or are you so popular that there's too many to count?" I tease.

Nate laughs again. "You do kind of get them all mixed up after a while! Let's see, I rushed Phi Psi, Theta Chi, Sig Ep, and Delta Rho which is where we're going. That's the one I got a bid to. Some guys I know who went to Resslar were in that frat and I didn't believe them when they told me it was the best group of guys, but I was wrong." He glances down at me as he swings our clasped hands back and forth. "What about you? Ever think of joining a sorority?"

"You know, I considered it. It seemed like every girl was doing it, so I looked into it, but it was too much money for me. Plus, I have a group of friends I like." I shrug. "The sorority girls were fun, but it's something I never really felt the need to do."

Nate nods in understanding. "I get it. Weirdly enough, it's something I *always* felt the need to do. Having a social life in college was a big thing for my brothers. I mean, they're always talking about the shit they'd do with their teammates. Guess I just want a family like that," he considers.

We pass the creepy frat house and as always, I get goosebumps regardless of the wind that's rustling my hair. Nate notices how I become silent and looks at me curiously.

"You okay?" he says.

"Yeah, I'm fine. That house is kind of creepy," I say truthfully. Nate looks over at it as we pass by and he smiles to himself.

"It really is. I never noticed it before." He looks at me with a raised eyebrow. "Want to take a closer look?"

I roll my eyes. "Thanks for the offer, but I'm not going near it. Not after that cop yelled at me when I walked on the porch," I tell him. Nate scoffs, and I giggle. "What?"

"C'mon, we both know you aren't the best at dropping anything. I mean, why pick fights with the asshole in COM134 or keep your unpaid job at a place where you're the youngest by far?" Nate laments sarcastically.

I laugh a little bit and shrug. "I don't know really. Maybe I have something to prove." I consider that as I walk. Nate's quiet as he lets me think. "My dad is obsessed with success and money and all of that. That's why my parents split. He was hoarding money from my mom and me." I hear Nate swallow. "He was happy I got into Resslar because it's a high-level school which puts me on a good path to become as successful as he is. He just wants me to win at everything I do. I don't let go of things with Taylor because that would let him win. My job at the station isn't just to impress other people, it's to make me feel like I've won something by being the youngest student there." I swallow hard. I've never been this introspective by myself before, let alone with a boy I just met. "Investigating things when I was a kid made me feel important, and it also made other people happy. I guess as I've gotten older, it's been more about me and making myself look better and more successful… and that's kind of awful to say." I scoff at myself as Nate comfortingly squeezes my hand.

"Not at all. Sometimes we have to do things for ourselves." He gives me a lopsided smile. I give his hand a little squeeze.

We round the corner, walk a few more feet up the road and then arrive at the Delta Rho house. It's a three-story thing that looks like cardboard boxes stacked haphazardly on top of one another. The pieces of dark blue siding that aren't falling off seem like they're the only things keeping the house together. Like every other house in the neighborhood, the windows are old, the steps are slightly crumbled, and there is a gravel driveway off to the side that's packed with cars. I can hear the bass vibrating from outside and see the colored lights through the window. There are a few other guys arriving with dates. Nate breathes out heavily then looks at me.

"Ready?" he asks. I have no choice but to nod. I'm here now and I couldn't back out if I wanted to. So, with Nate's arm locked with mine, we walk inside of the Delta Rho house.

When we enter, the smell of alcohol hits my nose like a freight train. The house lights are dimmed except for one brighter light coming from a room in the back of the house which I can only assume is the kitchen. As soon as I take another step, everything seems to slow down, and I can experience everything as though I'm hyper-aware. It seems like simply *entering* a frat house makes me feel like I'm under the influence of something.

Nate leads me past the girls dancing in the living room into the kitchen where some senior brothers are behind a table with random bottles on it. Solo cups are knocked over and some have spilled their contents everywhere.

The kitchen is packed with pledges and their dates. I wouldn't be able to make my way through if it wasn't for Nate in front of me. We stop at the table functioning as a bar where I see three boys talking loudly dressed in outfits similar to Nate's.

"Guys!" Nate says with a smile. The three boys turn to him and break out into laughter.

"Hey, it's Nate!" says one.

"We were wonderin' when you were gonna show!" says another. The third one shakes his hand then brings him in over the table to clap him on the back. I patiently stand to the side and let them reunite, taking a drink, sipping it and then wanting to spit it out. I don't drink much, but I've tasted enough to know that whatever is in the cup will burn my insides. I put the cup back down and begin to think of a way to get the taste out of my mouth.

"Guys, this is Brooklyn," Nate says, offering his hand out to me. I take it and step up to greet the guys.

"Nice to meet you," says the only one with brown hair. "Trent Andrews. Your boyfriend's a hell of a guy. Longest keg stand I've seen in a while."

"Aw you're just being nice," Nate says, waving him off.

"No seriously, best pledge ever," says the blonde one next to Trent. "I'm Dylan. Nice to meet you. Your name is sick!"

"My parents loved the borough, so they figured why not name their kid after it?" I say with a laugh. The three guys laugh with me.

"And this is Oliver," Nate says, motioning to the redhead behind the table. Oliver shakes my hand and nods his head at me.

"I love your dress," he compliments.

"Oh, thanks!" I say.

"Hey, we're gonna make a round. Pour me a drink though?" Nate asks. Trent grabs a few bottles and pours some of all of them into a cup then hands it to Nate. Trent winks as he hands it over.

"You're welcome in advance," he says. Trent looks at me. "Can I get anything for you?"

"Um a Vodka Cranberry?" I ask. After Oliver hands Trent the juice, Trent pours half of each ingredient and hands it to me. "Thanks!"

Nate and I walk through the house, saying hello to different members of the frat. I'm introduced, then re-introduced, then whisked away from people I just met. As the night goes on, the smells of stale beer and weed start to make my head hurt. I've been a spectator to too many games of Pong and too many guys have tried to hit on me instead of their date. In fact, most of the girls here are stumbling around trying to dance to the pounding music with their red cup in the air or grinding on their date. There are times where I lose Nate, then find him, then lose him again. Finally, I end up on the stairs outside the side door to the kitchen with a second cup of Vodka Cran, listening to the sounds of the bass drift lazily out of the cracks in the walls.

"Having fun?" says a dry voice behind me. I look up to see a tall gangly kid holding a cup of his own. He has dark red hair and an oval-shaped face with blazing blue eyes set far back in his skull. To frame them are glasses that look like they might fall down his slender nose at any moment.

"Yeah," I say half-heartedly as he sits down next to me. When he gets closer, I can see a small number of freckles dotting his flushed cheeks. "Are you?"

"The *most* fun," says the boy sarcastically, taking a sip of his drink. "Are you someone's date?"

"Nate's," I tell him. The boy widens his eyes.

"Wow. Lucky guy," the boy says.

"Thanks. I can't find him. He's in there somewhere." I gesture back to the house with my chin then look back down at my shoes.

"And *I've* lost *my* date! Cheers!" The boy knocks his cup against mine and takes a gulp as I snort to myself. "Sorry, what's your name?"

"Brooklyn. And yours?"

"Brendon."

"Nice to meet you."

"What year are you?" Brendon asks.

"Freshman," I tell him.

"Oh, good for you. What's your major?"

"Broadcast journalism. I'm in Rosenburg," I say.

"Oh, me too! Advertising!" Brendon looks off into the night sky like he's remembering something. "If only I was good enough to be a journalist. I'm crap at writing."

"Well, they teach you how to write," I reassure him.

"They teach you the *style* of writing. You have to know *how* to write in the first place," Brendon corrects. He takes another sip. "So, you must be pretty smart. How'd you meet a bonehead like Nate?"

"He's in my COM134 class," I explain.

"Gotcha." Brendon huffs. "Your boyfriend is quite the guy."

"What do you mean?"

"Every older brother in DR loves him. He's a shoo-in," Brendon sighs. "Guys like him make it harder for the rest of us."

"The whole rushing process is all politics as far as I'm concerned," I tell him.

"You're not wrong there," Brendon agrees. There's a pause before he goes on tentatively. "That kid though... he's, like, *too* perfect."

"How so?"

"Everything he does is just... I don't know, it's weird. My friend James Earl, he's in the frat already, he's the one who got me to rush. He said that Nate's dad is some big shot in the city. Says the guy has crazy money so of course, he sends Nate here. The jackass can buy his way into anything. And then once he's in, he does everything so perfectly. It's weird." I look at him with confusion. Brendon shakes his head. "I don't know, Nate just gives me a bad vibe sometimes. It's like he can do everything flawlessly because he has money. I know I just met you but I'm just gonna tell you up front: Don't let him buy you." I let his somewhat condescending speech sink in before I respond.

"He hasn't tried to buy me yet, so I think I'm in the clear," I reassure him. Brendon raises an eyebrow.

"Have you refused something he's given you?" he asks suspiciously.

"Well, no. I haven't known him for that long," I say.

Brendon nods and takes another drink. "Just wait for it. He always gets what he wants. And when it happens, tell me. James hasn't been wrong about anyone in this freaking house yet." Brendon finishes off his drink and gives me a smile. "See you later." The boy gets up and leaves me there on the stoop as I digest all the information that he just gave me. The ominous warning about not letting myself be bought is unsettling to think about. However, I don't think of myself as materialistic, so I should have nothing to worry about. Just as I'm about to dive in deeper, I'm stopped by the man of the hour.

"Hey, there you are! I've been looking for you!" Nate sits down next to me and clears a piece of hair out of my face.

"I just stepped outside to get some air," I say.

"Can't blame you for that one," laughs Nate. I give him a smile which turns to a sort of frown. Nate looks concerned and turns to fully face me. "Something wrong?" I shrug.

"I don't know. I don't think I'm cut out for the whole party scene. I mean, there's only so much vodka I can drink before I want to have some water." Nate laughs at me and tilts his head to the side as his eyes scan my face thoughtfully. I think for a second that he might kiss me, but instead he stands up and holds out his hand.

"C'mon Ms. Perce. I have somewhere to take you," he says in an official tone. I look at his hand and think about what Brendon told me about refusing an offer. I look up at Nate who's looking at me sneakily. I smile and take his hand, ready for whatever he wants to do.

We walk back down the street away from the vibrating house and the farther we get, the less I hear the driving bass. Our hands still stay locked as we walk back up the stairs to get to our dorms. On the way up the hill, I look at the night sky. Each star that I can see twinkles like a little flashlight.

"It's such a beautiful night," I say partially to myself. Nate looks up too.

"It really is." We don't say anything else until we get into his building. I watch him as he hits the button inside of the elevator to bring us to the top floor of Cypress. I look over at him with my eyes narrowed flirtatiously.

"I thought you lived on the fifth floor?" I say. Nate gives me a sly side-eye and doesn't say anything. We get off of the elevator and exit into the lounge of the tenth floor. Nate goes over to the stairwell beside the three elevators and eases open the door. He takes the stairs two at a time and gets to the door at the top. A sign on the metal says whatever's behind it is for authorized personnel only but Nate opens it anyway and no alarm sounds. The cold air from the outside rushes down the stairwell and I hug myself to keep the chill at bay as much as I can.

"What the hell?" I ask, coming up to the landing.

"Brooklyn Perce, I present to you the entire city of Northwich, New York," says Nate, sweeping his hand outwards. I slowly approach the door and then walk out onto the roof of Cypress.

From the tar rooftop, I can see the entire city stretch itself out below me with seemingly no end. The lights from the buildings blend beautifully into the horizon line. I can see far beyond the campus in all directions with the city to my north and the countryside to my south. I can't stop turning in a circle, taking it all in as the view fills my senses. When I look up to the sky, I can see the stars gleaming brightly in patterns I never could understand. I try to say something, but the view takes everything out of me. I see Nate come up to me out of the corner of my eye, and I turn to him with my hands over my mouth.

"What do you think?" he says proudly, stretching out his arms.

"It's amazing. How did you know you could get up here?" I ask him.

"A buddy at the house told me they don't lock the door. I come here whenever I feel overwhelmed. It's a good place to get away from everything going on down there." He gestures to campus which stretches out to the left. I keep looking around at the view as he's talking, my feet wandering around the rooftop. I make sure to stay far away from the edge since heights aren't really my thing. I finally decide to sit down so I face the skyline. My eyes let the lights blur, and I become hypnotized by the swimming specks of yellow.

"This is amazing," I say, running out of words to describe it. "Truly amazing." Nate sits beside me as I admire the view of the city. I put my head on his shoulder and he puts his arm around me.

"Hey Brooklyn?" whispers Nate after a few minutes of silence.

"Yeah?"

"Thanks for coming with me tonight."

I smile sheepishly. "Well thanks for inviting me," I respond quietly.

"Meet anyone interesting?" he asks.

"This kid named Brendon?"

Nate scoffs. "Isn't he fun?" he says sarcastically.

I chuckle along with him. "Sure is." We sit in silence again. "He told me to make sure you don't buy me."

Nate snorts again. "Of course he did." He sighs, heaving his shoulders up and down so my head moves. "One day I'll tell you about my dad. I don't feel like getting bummed out right now."

"Okay." I take his hand from his lap and am about to close my eyes when I feel him kiss the top of my head. I turn towards Nate and look him in the eyes, the light from the city reflecting in his amber irises. My heart pounds uncontrollably in my chest as he tucks my hair behind my ear, leaving his hand on the back of my head. Sure enough, Nate starts to kiss me and, as cliché as it sounds, time stops. My entire being melts into a blob, so I kiss him harder in order to feel like a solid human. I have to remind myself to breathe as we take turns kissing each other harder and harder until I become out of breath and I rest his forehead on mine.

"I'm freezing," I finally say. Nate's face breaks into a smile as he breathily laughs.

"Alright. Wanna go inside?" he asks.

I kiss him again. "In a minute."

❊ ❊ ❊

After I make out with Nate on the rooftop a few more times, I decide to go back to my building. On the walk over, I check my phone which tells me it's 2 a.m. No wonder I'm so tired.

I flash my Student I.D. at the C.P. officer who is guarding the front desk of Smith so he can see I live here, and I go up the three flights of stairs to get to my floor. I open and close the dorm room door as quietly as possible since Drew is asleep. Once I wash my face, brush my teeth, and change into my pajamas, I get in my bed and check my phone. There are a few texts from Drew just wondering what I'm up to and a couple from my group chat with my friends back home.

But then there's a picture message from an unknown number.

I swallow hard as I open up the pictures and I have to stop myself from screaming. The first photo is Nate and me on the roof with me lying on Nate's jacket on the gravel as he's on top of me as we kiss. There's another picture of me sitting in his lap, hands on his chest, kissing him. *How long was this person watching us?*

The only thing accompanying the three photos is a small message.

YOU DON'T STAY AWAY, WE DON'T EITHER.
DROP IT.

I rush over to my computer and open my laptop. Sure enough, I don't have to type in a password. Someone's been in my room. Drew must've forgotten to lock the door on her way out. When I open up Google Chrome, my search history has been cleared. I put my head in my hands and just stare at the computer screen. I frantically search in my desk for the paper that I took my notes on, but it's gone. When I open my mouth, meaning to cry out of terror, I can only say one word.

"Shit."

7

The next morning at breakfast, I stare at my omelet. I don't want to close my eyes because whenever I do, I see the text message I was sent last night. It's burned into my brain, and my mind is so fixated on it that it drowns out Drew's yapping. Kenni, however, is listening intently. Drew's been talking nonstop about the concert, and I only tune in for the end of the conversation when I hear Ryker's name.

"And, Brook, your friend Ryker? Holy *shit,* he's gorgeous. Where did he come from? He was *totally* hitting on me too, Kenni. You should've seen it. Did you know he travels? We talked about wanting to go to Antarctica the *entire* time before the show started. *And* he used to be a drummer in a band. It was in high school, but still." Drew pretends to melt, putting out her hands and arms flat on the table and throwing her head back. "Brook, I'm gonna hook up with your radio show boss. It's gonna happen." I just stare at her and blink a few times, trying to process the avalanche of information.

"Drew, I think he has a girlfriend," I finally tell her.

"Not by the way he was talkin' about you," Drew says, trying to not smile. Kenni glances from me to Drew. I cross my arms skeptically.

"What? You guys talked about me?" Drew nods.

"Oh sure. The guy was singing your praises. Kinda cute but also kinda annoying." Drew puts a grape in her

81

mouth and chews it thoughtfully. Kenni rips off a piece of her waffle and chews it as I debate bringing up what happened last night.

"Have you guys ever been stalked before?" I ask my friends slowly. Kenni's mouth drops.

"Um, why the hell would you ask us that?" she says.

"I just–I want to know. Have you?" I say. Drew raises an eyebrow.

"Sort of? After Max and I broke up, he had his friend follow me around. It only lasted a week until I came at the kid with my car and threatened to run him over if he kept following me." After Kenni and I give her surprised looks, Drew shrugs. "I was kidding of course." She casually eats another grape. "Why do you ask?"

"I don't know... I feel like somebody's watching me," I tell her.

Drew nods. "It's very possible. I mean, the government is watching us all the time." Kenni rolls her eyes.

"No, not like the government. Like a *student* is watching me," I whisper.

My roommate's plucked eyebrows crease. "What are you talking about?" I decide to take out my phone and show her the text from last night. "I got that after I came home yesterday." Drew takes the phone from me with a gaping mouth as she scrolls through the pictures. Kenni looks on and her eyes grow to the size of her plate.

"Okay, you look good, but that's horrific. Who's sending these to you?" she asks.

"Hell if I know!" I say. "Someone else called me after I went to WRDW the other night too." Drew's eyes get wider. "I didn't recognize the voice."

"What are they telling you to stay away from?" Kenni asks as Drew hands back my phone.

"That SHA frat house," I mutter.

Drew rolls her eyes. "You're *still* stuck on that? Brook, you gotta drop it if someone's going to come after you," she advises.

I groan. "Dude, I can't! There's a story there, and I just can't get away from it. It's weird. I have this…this *urge* to do something about it."

"An urge like a death wish?" Kenni says, not even caring that her coffee is getting cold.

"No! Not like that." I bite my lip. "That CP officer seemed keen on keeping me away from the house. Ever since then, I can't stop thinking about what happened to that place."

"Brooklyn, this needs to stop. You need to call the cops," Drew says in a final sort of way. "I mean, I don't normally mess with the cops, but this is serious stuff."

"The cops will only make it worse," I whisper.

"By doing what? Tracking the phone number and catching this weirdo?"

"No, the number can't be traced. I tried that this morning. Plus, the damn cops might be involved in covering this thing up."

Kenni's eyes get wider, so wide that I think they'll pop. "Why the hell would *that* thought cross your mind?"

"None of the investigations of the dead brother or of the journalist killing got anywhere."

"Could that be because—and bear with me here—that C.P. officers are *inept,* hence why they're not actual cops?" Drew muses.

"They got *real* cops on the case, Drew. And that's beside the point, I'm afraid that—" I stop mid-sentence as people pass us and continue when they leave. "I'm afraid this person is going to hurt me if I tell anyone."

Drew rolls her eyes. "So why are you telling us, Stupid?" she scolds, gesturing to her and Kenni.

"Because I think Nate has something to do with it!" I blurt out. Drew's eyebrows get closer together. Kenni looks off into the distance as if she's calculating the probability of what I just said.

"The plot thickens." Drew slurps her drink. "Explain."

"I met this kid Brendon at that party last night who said Nate gave him the creeps."

"How so?" Kenni asks.

"Brendon basically said Nate can buy anything he wants because his father's this big wig in the city. The kid said Nate's life seemed to be too perfect, like he had everything planned."

"Okay, so what does this have to do with the frat house?"

I shrug in answer to her question. "Maybe he's trying to keep me away from it for some reason," I guess. "Maybe he's getting closer to me to distract me from the house." Drew leans back into the cushioning of the booth, considering it.

"Doesn't Finn not like frats either? Who's to say it's not him sending you these?" Kenni asks. Now Drew looks offended.

"*Finn*? The same Finn who got chased by a goose on the Quad?" Drew scoffs.

"What's a goose got to do with anything?" Kenni questions.

"I'm just saying, the kid ran from a *goose*. You think he's got the balls to go after a *person*?" Drew says, her voice becoming more high-pitched.

"Geese are mean, so he was smart to run, but Drew's right. Finn's not vengeful. If something happened that made him angry, he would rather talk about it than give death threats," I say.

Kenni bites her fingernail. "I don't know, I feel like there are a lot of things he doesn't tell us. I mean, think of how mad he gets whenever you mention that frat house."

"It's not Finn," Drew says definitively.

Kenni shakes her head. "You never know. He hates frats, he's always weird whenever you bring it up. He could be wrapped up in this somehow." There's a pause where I let that sink in. There's no way Finn would harm me, his friend. Drew sits back in her chair and crosses her arms.

"You know, if we're going with this crazy theory, I'm re-molding that bust of him today for class. I could feel him out for you," offers Drew.

"Thanks, but just sculpt for now. I don't want anyone else knowing about this. Keep this between us, okay?" I ask her. Drew nods reassuringly.

"Of course, of course. I don't want you dying on my watch. Although I did hear that if your roommate dies, you get straight A's for the rest of the semester, so your death might be taking one for the team," Drew jokes.

I laugh weakly.

※ ※ ※

I go to the radio station that day hoping that someone needs help with a project. Drew tags along to hand over her SD card full of pictures to Ryker. I told her I was more than capable of giving him a little chip, but she insisted, claiming that 'seeing his beautiful face' would brighten her day.

I swipe my card and enter the station, the inside of which would be silent had it not been for Lukas and Syd chatting in the lobby.

"Yeah, the new album is sick," Syd says in a voice that indicates she's probably indifferent about the album.

"Honestly, the last one is better. This one just seems like a random assortment of songs, not like the last one that tells an actual story." Syd glances over his shoulder at me. When Lukas turns and sees me. "Oh hey. He's in there." Lukas motions for me to go into the newsroom where I find Ryker sitting with his feet up on the desk, computer in his lap. He turns around, and I see Drew wilt with a sigh.

"Hey, it's Brooklyn!" says my boss, breaking into a smile. He shuts the lid to his laptop rather violently. "Dropped by to say hi?"

"We weren't doing anything, so I was wondering if you needed any help," I say causally. Ryker takes his feet off of the desk, looks around, and shakes his head, his brown hair sort of falling into his eyes. I can see Drew trying not to swoon.

"No, I think I've got everything covered here. But you have something for me, don't you?" Ryker asks my roommate, giving her a smile. Drew just stares at him for a second, batting her eyes while processing his question, then clears her throat.

"Oh yeah, yeah, here's the SD card. I got a lot of pictures, but I deleted the ones that were blurry or had bad lighting. You can just sort through the ones you like," she says, handing over the card into Ryker's open hand.

"Sweet. I'll take a look at 'em when I write my story later," he tells her, pocketing the card.

"What are you writing now?" I ask.

"Oh nothing, just an essay for a class," he waves off.

"What class?" Drew asks sweetly.

"One of my Rosenburg classes. Stupid stuff, really doesn't mean much," Ryker says. He looks at Drew. "That concert was something else, huh?"

Thrilled that he's addressing her, Drew perks up. "For my first time shooting a concert, yeah! I was internally freaking out," Drew rambles.

"It was really cool. And Young Yesterday was even better live than on Spotify," Ryker adds.

"The only problem was I was trying to see over you the entire time," Drew flirtatiously jabs.

"Well, if you weren't shorter than me, you wouldn't have that problem," Ryker says with a wink. I try not to roll my eyes. Watching the world's best flirts go at it is truly something

Drew scoffs and crosses her arms. "I've tried growing. It just doesn't work," she complains mockingly.

Ryker pretends to think. "Well at the next concert, I'll have to put you on my shoulders," he says.

Drew looks taken aback. "*Next* concert?" she says.

Ryker nods and hands her his phone. "Yeah. Put your number in, and I'll call you the next time I want you to shoot a concert. Your pictures would be in our online stuff. You could be a contributing photographer," he says.

Drew eagerly puts her number into the phone. "That would be awesome!" she says excitedly.

"Yeah, I'll just text you. Sound good?" he asks.

"Sounds fantastic," Drew says, staring into Ryker's baiting eyes. He has a knowing smirk on his face like he's luring her into a trap.

"We should be going," I step in, dragging Drew away from Ryker and effectively breaking whatever it is they have going on.

"Yeah I'll see you this week, Brooklyn! Bye Drew," Ryker says, giving my roommate an award-winning smile.

"Bye," Drew says faintly. Once we walk out of the newsroom and out of the front door, Drew starts to skip down the sidewalk. When she gets to the corner where we cross the street, she turns around with a mega-watt smile on her face.

"I have his number," she sings happily.

"I'm proud of you," I tell her.

"And I'm a contributing photographer!" Drew runs across the street not looking out for cars and sighs when she gets to the other side. "It's been a great day already, and it's only two in the afternoon."

Drew keeps talking about Ryker's rugged, yet slightly nerdy good looks as we walk down the street towards the back stairs. As we pass the SHA house, I start to walk towards it, veering off of the sidewalk and onto the back lawn. Drew jogs a bit to catch up to me.

"This is the frat house?" Drew asks warily, looking at the damaged facade. I nod and stare up at it, my eyes taking in every detail. "This is creepy as hell." I walk up on the back porch, the old concrete cracked and crumbled into pieces beneath my feet. There's a sheet of plywood where the window on the door used to be and the knob has been replaced with a bolt so no one can get inside. I put my hand on the rusted bolt and for a second, my brain wonders if I could twist it open.

"Brooklyn, c'mon," Drew says urgently.

"Yes, get off of the porch please." A condescending voice makes me whip around. It's the same C.P. officer who caught me checking out the house the first time. He raises a bushy yet kept eyebrow and chomps on his gum. "We can't keep meeting like this," he says sarcastically.

"I told her to get off of the porch," Drew tells him. I stare into the cop's eyes, and he scoffs.

"Your friend is clearly smarter than you are," he says to me. "Now, get the hell down from there." Not breaking eye contact, I jump off of the porch and land in front of the cop. The officer smirks. I can see now that he's actually a young guy with dark features and a hard jawline with stubble on it. He seems built for his age. His badge says Officer Roger Greenwood.

"What are you doing? I thought I told you to not trespass here," Greenwood snaps.

"What happened to the fraternity that was here?" I snap back. I see Drew look at me with a shocked expression.

Greenwood raises his eyebrows. "*Excuse* you?" he asks, clearly telling me to watch my tone.

I break eye contact with the cop and clear my throat. "Sorry," I say.

Greenwood nods. "What's your name?"

"Brooklyn Perce," I tell him.

"Alright *Brooklyn Perce,* you're clearly unresponsive to authority, so I'll make this clear." Greenwood leans in and narrows his eyes. "If I catch you here again, I will make sure you're brought up on trespassing charges. Got it?"

"Yes." I try not to say it though my teeth.

"Yes what?"

"Yes, *Sir,*" I growl unwillingly.

Greenwood smiles smugly. "Good. Now leave." He looks at Drew. "Same goes for you. Get out." Drew quickly nods and runs back to the sidewalk, but I linger to look at the officer. He looks approvingly at the house, then senses I'm looking at him. Greenwood's head whips around and I freeze. "Was I not clear? Leave!" he shouts. That snaps me out of it. I run back to the sidewalk and keep walking, feeling the cop's eyes burn holes in my back.

"Holy shit, that was horrifying," Drew whispers, slowing down to look back at Greenwood. I shake my head.

"Keep walking," I say confidently. Drew falls back into step with me. She's having some difficulty as I walk at a brisker pace than usual.

"How can you be this sure of yourself when you just got chewed out by an officer?" she hisses, looking ahead like I told her.

"The way he was looking at me and the tone of his voice tells me I was too close to something."

"Yeah. *The house,*" Drew says with a timid laugh.

"I need to find out what happened to that place," I say defiantly.

"Need I remind you that you have a stalker on your tail who doesn't seem like he's friendly," Drew says, sounding like a nagging younger sibling.

"Alright," I shrug with an air of anger. We get to the front door of our building, and I turn around to face her. Drew looks scared for me. I've never seen her like this before, and it's unsettling. "Drew, I have to figure this out or it'll haunt me forever."

Drew sighs. "Well, if you're gonna dedicate your life to this, I might as well dedicate the rest of mine to it too," she says. My lips break into a smile. Drew huffs and crosses her arms. "Alright, don't get so happy about it," she says. "If I die, it's your fault."

"You're not going to die."

"Alright, sure, but let's hypothetically say I die. That's on you."

※ ※ ※

"So, what are we doing?" Drew asks loudly in the library that night. We get a few dirty looks from other students which prompts her to roll her eyes. "What are we doing?" she repeats in an exaggerated whisper.

"Learning as much as we can about fraternities," I say, opening my laptop and typing 'history of fraternities' into Google. "Recruitment, hazing, membership dues, all of that."

"And why did we come to the library if we're just gonna Google things?" Drew asks. I gesture vaguely to the numerous shelves of books to our left.

"Personal history of Resslar frats," I clarify.

Drew nods approvingly. "Smart." She types something into her laptop, clicks on something, then starts taking notes. For almost two hours we sit in the library, learning everything there is to know about Greek life. When I start to read about hazing events and traumatic occurrences within different frats at different

91

schools, it makes me feel sick, yet I can't tear my eyes away from the screen. It's like watching a train wreck in slow motion.

After I finish reading about Penn State and their entire fraternity crisis, I get the all too familiar uneasy feeling that I'm being watched. I flick my eyes up from my computer and slyly look around. Everyone's heads are still buried in their work. No one seems to be paying us any attention, except the librarian who surveys everyone with a watchful glare.

"Pst. Brook," Drew whispers, looking over my shoulder. My eyebrows crease in confusion. Drew shakes her head slightly. "Don't turn around." I pretend to be stretching my back so I can glance over my shoulder as I twist. Sure enough, there's a boy there staring directly into my back. He has on black Beats headphones that match his black laptop case which matches his black sweatshirt. The boy is staring directly at me. I gulp and turn around.

"Maybe we should—"

"For sure." Drew and I quickly pack up our things and leave, the boy watching us the entire way.

8

"Okay, what's your biggest regret?" I'm quizzing Nate before our COM class. We're sitting in the cafe in Rosenburg eating and chatting. I'm having a turkey sandwich with lettuce, cheese, and mustard while Nate is eating a wrap with pork in it and sipping a smoothie. Hundreds of kids have passed us, but the only person I notice is my boyfriend.

"Probably taking those Irish Step Dancing lessons," Nate says after a moment of thinking. I snort since merely thinking of an All-American boy in an Irish Step Dancing outfit is hilarious. "They were fun, but useless other than the footwork part. Now you. What's your biggest fear?" I swallow the bite of the sandwich and wipe some mustard off of my lips.

"I hate the idea of falling from a height," I tell him, shuddering at the thought of being stranded on the tippy top of One World Trade Center and then plummeting into the concrete below. Nate chuckles and takes another bite of his wrap. "What's your favorite color?" Nate raises an eyebrow.

"I thought I told you already," he says. I shake my head.

"Nope. What's your favorite color, Stevenson?" I ask again. Nate laughs to himself again. He looks into my eyes and he seems like he's studying them.

"It's this green color. Not like the color of grass but the color of a new leaf on a tree. And the color is kind of translucent. Like, you can see right through it if you tried." I shake my head and smile. Nate laughs. "Have you caught on yet?" I nod.

"Mmhmm," I say, biting my lip. "You're sweet."

"What's yours?"

"A pale blue. Sort of like a robin's egg color." I look at my phone and widen my eyes. "We should go if we want to be on time for class." Nate nods and the two of us get up to throw away our trash. I sling my bag over my shoulder, and we make our way to the lecture hall. In the stairwell, Nate grabs my wrist and spins me around.

"Hey!" I exclaim, caught off guard. Nate quickly plants a kiss on my lips and smiles.

"Okay, now we can go," he says, going down the stairs in front of me. I roll my eyes, but there's a smile on my face.

We arrive at the lecture hall and stand in the crowd of our peers, waiting for the other class to get out. I notice everyone's on their phones, but Nate and I are standing there holding hands. I quickly make eye contact with Taylor who smirks and begins to saunter over to us. I turn away, take my hand away from Nate's, and tuck my hair behind my ear. My leg starts to nervously bounce in place. Nate notices the change in my mood and he's about to ask me what's wrong when Taylor approaches.

"Hey Stevenson," snaps Taylor bitterly. Nate sticks his tongue in his cheek and looks at Taylor with his upper lip twitching. Taylor glares at me with a smile. "And look, it's my favorite journalism major."

I give him a tight fake smile as I fight off the urge to give the patronizing asshole the finger.

"What do you want Taylor?" Nate sighs.

"I want to know how an asshole like you gets a bid to Delta Rho, but I don't," Taylor interrogates.

"Because you're awful," I say, snapping to my boyfriend's defense. Taylor looks taken aback for a second, then sneers.

"Brooklyn can bite," he mutters with a laugh. "Can't fight your own battles, huh Stevenson? Need the girl to do it for you?" I give him a sneer and cross my arms. Taylor scoffs at me and then turns back to Nate. "Tell me why, Stevenson."

"I can't tell you a reason," Nate says simply. "Maybe the brothers just like me better than you."

"Bullshit. Tell me why," Taylor demands. Nate shrugs in response. "My dad's gonna kick my ass if I don't get in. That's his frat."

"Well Taylor, maybe your dad *should* kick your ass. It might knock some sense into you." As soon as the sentence leaves Nate's mouth, Taylor's hands jump at Nate's throat. I scream and clasp my hands over my mouth, attracting the attention of everyone in the hallway. Nate grabs onto Taylor's wrists and pries Taylor's hands off of his neck. He shoves Taylor backwards, but Taylor goes at him again. Nate puts up his arms, protecting his face.

"Hey!" I shout. Taylor turns around, murder in his eyes. Without thinking, I take my right hand, make a fist, and punch him in the cheek. Taylor's head whips to the right as my classmates collectively gasp. My hand aches. Nate, who's still against the wall, stares at me in disbelief as Taylor nurses his bruising cheek. I can see some blood pool in the space between his front lip and his gums as he glares at me with a partially opened mouth.

"You bitch," snarls Taylor. He shoots a look at Nate then looks at me. His gaze cuts me like a knife as he seems to be debating whether or not to lose all of his dignity and hit a girl. When he realizes everyone is watching, he decides against it. He bares his teeth and chuckles, his fists clenching at his sides. Taylor gives me one final vengeful look, then leaves the hallway, students parting like the Red Sea to let him through.

As everyone files into COM class, Nate takes the seat next to me that Taylor would've sat in. Nate's mouth is wide open as I take out my notebook and pen. My hand is still shaking, and my veins are still be pumped with adrenaline, but I try not to let it show. I throw my hair over my shoulder and look straight ahead at the slideshow my professor is loading. Nate hasn't moved.

"Okay, are we just going to ignore that you just punched that kid?" Nate whispers incredulously.

"He was gonna *strangle* you Nate! Over a freaking *fraternity bid*!" I hiss back as the professor starts talking.

"Brooklyn, he's going to murder you," Nate says.

"No, he's not. If he wants another chance to rush 'his frat' in the spring, he won't want to get expelled because he killed someone," I reason, writing down the notes on the slideshow. Nate still hasn't gotten his books out. He's just staring at me in awe.

"You're unbelievable," he finally says after a minute of silence. Nate kisses me on the cheek, takes out his laptop, and starts to type notes, shaking his head. "Un-freaking-believable."

Unraveling

✴ ✴ ✴

I walk home from class with Nate, checking over my shoulder every so often. He lightly holds my hand as we go up the stairs on our way back to our dorms.

"You know, I've never had a girlfriend who stood up for me before," Nate ponders. "I've always had to stand up for them."

"You did the same for me the first day I met you," I remind him. "I'm just repaying the favor." He squeezes my hand lovingly.

We reach the top of the stairs and walk to the front of my building where Nate kisses me goodbye before continuing to walk to Cypress. I go into Smith and up the stairs to my room where Drew is sitting at her desk typing up notes from her psychology lecture.

"Hey, how was class?" she asks.

"Good. I punched Taylor," I say casually. Drew chokes on the bit of water she just sipped from her bottle. She swivels around in her chair as she tries to swallow the rest of the water that's not dripping down her chin.

"You *punched* the asshole in your COM class?" she screams. I nod proudly. Drew shrieks and jumps up from her chair. "You're kidding me!"

"Drew, you should've seen it. He was going to strangle Nate over not getting into Delta Rho. When Taylor turned around, I punched him in the cheek." Drew is still silent.

"Just like that? You just–?" She punches the air halfheartedly with her first.

"Yeah. It felt really good to be honest with you," I say, setting down my bag and opening my laptop on my desk.

"That's...wow," Drew says.

"Now I have probably have two people who want to kill me on my tail," I joke with a half-hearted chuckle. Drew sits back down in her chair, still floored.

"I don't know what to say other than congratulations," she says.

The next day, I'm sitting in Finn's room doing homework with him and Kenni. It seems like whenever we do homework together, all of us become productive. I'm working on an assignment for my journalism class, Kenni is doing a report, and God knows what Finn is doing on his computer on the other side of the room. I'm sitting on his roommate's bed, and Kenni is on a bouncy chair in the middle of the room.

"Brooklyn, I heard you punched a guy," Finn says out of the blue.

Kenni turns to me with her mouth wide open. "Who did you punch?" she exclaims.

"This jerk in my COM class named Taylor. He was trying to choke out Nate because he didn't get into Delta Rho, so when he turned around, I punched him," I recount. "Who told you, Finn?"

"I'm friends with a guy in that class. He saw you do it."

"Look at that. You have fans," Kenni jokes.

Finn snorts. "That's freaking amazing, Brook. I wish I was there to see it," he muses.

"I didn't know your pure little self knew *how* to punch," Kenni says.

I shrug. "I've never punched someone before, but when it comes time to hit someone, you just automatically know how to do it," I say, shrugging like it's the darndest thing.

"Brooklyn the Bad Ass," Finn says jokingly, nodding approvingly. "I wish I could hit my roommate from time to time."

"You'd murder him!" I say, looking at Finn's biceps. Finn bares his teeth in a knowing smile.

"Not my fault that he's not as strong as me," he laughs. I laugh along weakly. The three of us turn back to our work. I'm done with my journalism assignment, and I'm texting Nate as I'm looking online for the location of the C.P. records office. There has to be one and I just have to figure out where.

Kenni gets up and goes to the door. "I'm gonna run to the bathroom," she says. As she's going by, she glances at my screen. "What are you looking at?"

"Nothing," I say, quickly clicking over to the CNN tab I have open.

"Why are you on the C.P. site?" Kenni asks with narrowed eyes.

"I wasn't. Stop snooping," I say. Kenni gives me a look calling my bluff but goes to the bathroom anyway, leaving Finn and I alone. I'm getting nothing on the C.P. site. All of a sudden, I have an idea. My eyes flick up to the unsuspecting orphaned boy sitting in front of me. His parents were supposedly in Greek life.

It's a long *long* shot.

But just maybe...

I take a deep breath and blow it out loudly through my mouth.

"All good?" Finn asks.

"Can I ask you a personal question? Like *really* personal," I emphasize.

Finn's eyes narrow. "Depends. What do you want to know?" he asks slowly.

"Where did you get adopted from?" I say after a beat. Finn just stares at me with his mouth open. I shake my head when the silence becomes too much. "Sorry, it's a stupid question."

"Why are you interested?" Finn asks.

"I'm doing a story about local orphanages for class, and I was just wondering if the name of yours popped up in my research at all." I thank God that I'm somewhat good at bullshitting.

Finn looks uncomfortably down at his keyboard. "Why are you doing a story about that?" he asks.

"We had to pick random story topics out of a hat, and I got orphanages," I say.

Finn snorts and stretches his arms up in the air. "Pretty convenient, huh?" he asks me sneakily, giving me a knowing look. I smile sheepishly and run my hand through my hair. "What's really the reason?"

"I told you, I have to write a story about it!" I say again. Finn bites his lip and avoids making eye contact with me. He looks like he's deciding whether or not to tell me. After a minute of silence, Finn finally meets my gaze.

"Lakewood Orphanage," he finally says. "It's a town or two over from Northwich. I've lived up here my whole life." I make a note of the orphanage on my laptop.

"Have you tried looking into your biological records?" I ask.

Finn raises his eyebrows. "You need this for a *story*, or are you asking because you're curious?" he questions back.

"Maybe a bit of both," I say in the most convincing voice I can.

Finn stretches his arms up over his head again. He shrugs. "I mean, my adopted family told me everything I needed to know about my biological parents. They didn't want me, so I don't want them. I'm actually perfectly fine going through life knowing only what my adopted parents told me about my biological ones. From what I know, they seemed like they were dicks, and they clearly were. They threw their son in an orphanage and scarred him for life because they didn't want him."

"If there's a chance they're alive though, wouldn't you want to meet them?" I ask him kindly.

"No. I'm actually happy I didn't know them. I love my adopted parents. *They're* my real family, not those assholes who gave me up then took off." There's silence after his little rant. I don't know what to say to that. I wish I could tell him the real reason for my asking, but I don't want to put one of my best friends in danger. In the middle of me feeling bad for lying, Kenni comes back and sits in her chair.

She whistles under her breath. "Yikes. Why's everyone so quiet?" she asks.

"Because there's no conversation without you, Kenni," I quickly compliment.

Kenni puts her hand over her heart. "Aw, you're so sweet. You go from hitting a guy in the face to hitting me in the heart," she says. Finn laughs at her and the tension is broken. The heaviness in my chest lifts a little.

I quickly research the orphanage and write down the phone number, thinking of lies I could tell the staff members in charge of records in order to get the names of Finn's biological parents. I could just ask Finn, but I don't have a good enough reason to ask for their names, and I don't want to invade his privacy any more than I already have. I know he's touchy with anything regarding his biological parents and I don't want to push it.

When I finish my homework, I say goodbye to Kenni and Finn and set off to Nate's room. He lives on the fifth floor, so I go down two flights of stairs and make a left coming out of the stairwell. I find the door with his name on it and take another deep breath. Once I knock on the door, I consider turning around and going home, but Nate answers the door too quickly.

"Hey, look who it is," he says. "C'mon in. What brings you to Cypress?"

"Visiting Finn," I say, stepping over a pair of shoes on the floor. Nate's roommate is out, but that side of the room is much messier than the side I'm on. Nate has kept his side relatively clean, but there are still sweatshirts on the floor and books stacked up on the desk. Nate kicks another pair of shoes out of my path so I don't trip. "What are you up to?"

"I was doing some homework until you knocked and gave me a nice excuse to stop," he laughs. Nate turns around and puts his hands on my waist. He goes in to kiss me but stops. "Is something wrong? You seem…off." I put down my bag and smooth down my shirt.

"Wrong? No, nothing's wrong," I say with a toothy smile.

Nate rolls his eyes. "You're a horrible liar," Nate laughs. He sits down on his bed. "C'mon tell me. What's up?" I look at my lap and twiddle my thumbs. I already took a risk telling Drew and if anything happened to Nate, I don't know what I would do. Nate sits down beside me and takes my hand. "Brooklyn, what's wrong?"

"Nate, I can't tell you," I say softly, looking up at my boyfriend with worried eyes. "I don't want you to get hurt."

Nate's face becomes concerned. "What are you talking about? No one's going to hurt me," Nate says, putting an arm around my shoulders. He looks into my eyes. The flirty look he had is gone. "Brooklyn, what is it?" I swallow hard and shake my head.

"Nate I—I can't tell you," I repeat, sadly looking into my boyfriend's eyes. After a second, Nate nods and looks at his lap.

"Alright. If you ever want to tell me, I'll be here. You know that, right?" Nate asks. I nod and put my head on his shoulder. Nate kisses the top of my head and holds me close to him. "I love you, Brooklyn." My heart sinks. That's the first time he's ever said that.

"I love you too, Nate," I say, turning to kiss him on the lips before putting my head back on his shoulder. I sit like that for what seems like an hour until I feel safe again, Nate hugging me the entire time.

❋ ❋ ❋

When I return to my dorm room, I flop onto my bed and take a big breath. If Finn is related to someone in the SHA frat, that would be simultaneously the best and worst thing ever.

The orphanage is closed, but I'll call later to see if they'll give me Finn's file. That's when I realize my sticky situation: Finn might have to call himself, but if I make him call for me that's one more person I have to tell about my potential murderer. I decide I should also call C.P. to see if I can access their records. I think I can since FERPA allows campus police records to be public like police documents. I shut my eyes and groan. This is all too much. When I decide to stand up, I immediately stumble backwards. Drew is in the doorway.

"Jesus, you scared me!" I exclaim.

Drew puts her hands up in surrender. "Sorry, I'll be sure to knock next time I enter *our* room," she jokes, putting down her backpack. "I met this cute guy in class today. Name's Dex. He says he has a minor in Rosenburg, but he's a junior. Do you know him?"

I shrug. "Never heard of him, but I'm happy for you." As she unpacks her things, I go to sit at my desk. "So, I asked Finn where he was adopted from and turns out, he's from the orphanage off of Route 81."

Drew shakes her head. "Brook…" she says in a warning tone.

"I'm going to look into it. It's a start! Could you *imagine* how nuts it would be if Finn's real parents were connected to this somehow?"

"So we're stalking our friend now?" Drew quips.

"Not stalking. I'd call it… *looking into* our friend," I rephrase. Drew jumps up onto her bed and sighs. "I'm calling C.P. tomorrow. Hopefully, they'll tell me something about the murder. In the meantime, I'm gonna call the orphanage that Finn was adopted from." Drew widens her eyes.

"You *sure* that's a good idea?" she questions.

I shake my head. "No, but it's the best lead I have," I say. When Drew still doesn't seem convinced, I keep talking. "Look Drew, I *know* it's a long shot, but what if he's somehow involved?"

"And what if you find his parents?"

"Then, I'm going to ask them if they know anything about what happened here."

"Brooklyn, there is literally a one in a million chance that Finn's parents went to this school, and there's a one in a *billion* chance that they would even know of the murder or know someone involved!" Drew sighs.

"If I don't look into it and it turns out to lead to something, I'll never forgive myself. I have to look at every possible option before determining if our friend wants to kill me," I say. Drew snorts.

"Alright calm down Nancy Drew, Finn would *never* hurt any of us," Drew says.

I roll my eyes. "Of course, you'd defend him, Drew! You like the kid! Look, I'm calling that orphanage and the C.P. office, and I'm figuring out what happened to that house because even though they closed the case, I think it's still very much open. I'll be damned if the questions I have go unanswered!"

"Why are you so paranoid about this?" Drew asks. It's not with malice, but with a genuine curiosity. I lean against my bed and cross my arms.

"I honestly can't explain it. Like I said, it's this odd urge that I have. I don't think I'll ever let it go until I figure it out. I mean, *cops* couldn't figure this out…or they didn't want to…and I want to know why." After my answer, Drew just scoffs with a smile on her face.

"I don't love Finn," she says.

"I didn't say 'love', I said 'like'," I say, trying to contain a smile. I go to my laptop that's sitting on my desk and open up my email. I see Ryker has emailed me an assignment that I have to return to him in two hours.

"Either. I don't like or love Finn," murmurs Drew as she grabs her laptop and types away madly. I shake my head, put in my headphones, and get to writing.

10

Today's Wednesday.

Wednesday means COM class.

COM class means seeing Taylor.

I take my seat and Nate takes his in front of me. He turns around and gives me a tight smile. I cross my arms and prop them on the table, looking over my shoulder to see if Taylor is coming. My leg is shaking, and I've lost the ability to sit still. Nate reaches across the small aisle to take my hand. I jump when he calmly puts his palm on top of mine.

"It'll be okay," Nate reassures me.

"Nate, I punched him in the face," I say nervously. Nate chuckles.

"Yeah you did." I give him a sad smile, my heart pounding faster and faster with every second. "How are you feeling about that now?"

"Not as good, I gotta say," I tell him.

"You want me to sit next to you?" he offers.

"No. I need to face him at some point." Nate nods in understanding, squeezes my hand once, then let's go. Just as he turns around, a fuming Taylor sits next to me. I suddenly become invested in the blank sheet of notebook paper I just turned to. I hear Taylor snicker.

"Hey Brooklyn," he sneers. Biting the bullet, I turn slowly to look at Taylor. I have to fight back a gasp.

When I punched him, I clearly didn't know my own strength. There is a purple, blue, black, and green mess between his cheek and his eye. He—or someone—has tried to cover it up with concealer or foundation, but it's poorly done so the bruise is exaggerated further. The thing protrudes out of his skull with such a force that I can't not look at it.

Taylor scoffs. "It'd be so easy to strangle you," he says wistfully. I gulp and open my mouth to say something, but no words come out. "I'm gonna leave you in suspense as to when I'm going to get you, Perce, but I'll make you pay for messing up my face."

"Taylor, I'm so sorry," I manage. Taylor gets dangerously close to me and the bruise becomes more pronounced. I swallow hard.

"I'm sure you are, you little bitch." He's too close for comfort, but I stare him down and look him in his soulless grey eyes.

"What else do you want from me? I said I was sorry," I say, searching his eyes and backing up a bit. The professor starts talking and doesn't seem to realize that Taylor is about a foot away from my face. It's like I'm about to get into a fight with an angry bulldog. In fact, I can almost see drool emerging from the corners of his mouth.

The shit-eating grin that erupts on Taylor's face makes me want to vomit. "I don't want anything from you. Yet," he spits. I gulp and turn back to my paper, but Taylor grabs my wrist and digs in his fingertips. I make a little sound of distress, causing Nate to turn only halfway around so he can't see what Taylor is doing. "Watch your back, Perce," he growls through his teeth. I look at him in horror, genuinely terrified. My legs are shaking, adrenaline compelling me to run.

"Let go," I say in a strong voice.

"Taylor!" My professor has finally noticed. Taylor immediately lets me go and turns to the front, his face innocent. "Everything alright?"

"Yes, Sir," says Taylor like an angel. He throws a final dirty look at me before scratching the words on the screen into his notebook. I quickly stand up, take my bag, push past his seat, and leave the classroom, my professor not even caring.

I sprint into the nearby stairwell and sink against the wall, my bag crashing off of my shoulder. The sound echoes off of the cinder block as I try to control my breathing. I feel like I'm going to throw up, but I try to suppress it. I put my head between my knees and start to rock back and forth. My entire body is shaking as my mind tries to calm itself down. Taylor couldn't be serious about wanting to strangle me. That's just not possible.

He is *about fifty pounds bigger than you. And he's* way *stronger than you are.* Then another thought comes to mind.

What if Taylor isn't kidding because he's the one who's been calling me and texting me?

What if he really has the means to kill me?

It's then I throw my bag over my shoulder, run up the stairs, into the bathroom, and throw up my guts into the sink. My jaw is trembling as I stare down at my own vomit. Everything is silent besides my heaving breaths.

"Pull yourself together," I whisper to my reflection in the mirror as I stand there shaking. I feel cold and clammy. Sweat is pouring down my forehead. I turn on the faucet to try to wash my partially digested breakfast down the sink.

The possibility that I could die hasn't hit me until now. I could actually be gone. I could leave my mom and my dad and my dog on this earth and cease to exist. They would ship my body back home and have a funeral for me. Kids from my high school would post about me online about that one time they talked to me and how I was a good person. Ma and Dad would stand on opposite sides of the grave as they lowered me inside my coffin down into the hole made of dirty and clay. Dad would be trying to hold it together, but Ma would be sobbing. They would say a prayer or two, recite a eulogy, and go home. I would be forgotten just like that.

I look in the mirror at my hazy green eyes and my quivering lips. My hair is in a mess all around my face. My cheeks are flushed. I swallow hard and pop a piece of gum into my mouth. I try to breathe in and out at a measured pace. After about five minutes of concentrated breathing, I decide I can leave the bathroom.

My feet carry me to a cushy chair in Newsworthy Cafe and my exhausted body sinks down into it. I watch people pass by me, staring at their happy faces. Something inside me becomes jealous at how carefree they seem. By taking on this SHA case, I've become suspicious and untrusting. I don't know what time it is, and I don't care. I'm happy I got out when I did. I could've been sitting next to a murderer in that class. Every moment next to him goes by as if in slow motion.

"Brooklyn!" It's Nate's voice that snaps me out of my funk. I stand up and my boyfriend bombards me with a hug. I grip him tightly and bury my face in his shoulder, my heartbeat instantly slowing itself down. Nate lets go and he looks into my eyes. "Are you okay?"

"Nate, I'm sorry I ran out. Taylor scared me, and he threatened to strangle me and if you knew what I was researching, you would know that I had to take that threat literally and now I'm facing the fact that I could die and I'm just–" Nate holds up his hands.

"Whoa, whoa, whoa Brooklyn. Slow down. You think you're going to *die*? Because of *Taylor*?" he asks, clearly not understanding a word I'm saying. My eyes flit around at the people who pass us. I take him by the hand quietly and lead him outside to a table in the corner of the little courtyard outside of the cafe. I wordlessly sit down. Nate puts his backpack down and looks at me with intense eyes. "Okay, tell me what the hell is going on." I swallow hard and look around to confirm there's no one around.

"You know that frat house on the corner that's abandoned?" I say softly. Nate nods.

"The SHA house, sure. What about it?"

"A brother died in the nineties and that's why the school banned the house. It was a murder and they don't know who did it. And I think my friend Finn is somehow involved in it." Nate raises his eyebrows.

"You're trying to find out who killed this guy back then?" he reiterates.

I nod. "And that's not even the worst part. There was a student journalist who looked into the story. He tried digging to go further than what C.P. said about it." I swallow hard as the headlines and photos of the journalist flash through my mind. "Nate, he was killed too." Nate's eyes look like they might pop out of his skull.

"*What?*" he whispers with a mix of shock and horror.

"He disappeared for two days before the cops found him dead on the front lawn," I say. Nate stares at me, his disbelieving expression permanently pasted onto his face. "There was another journalist who reported on the journalist's death and none of the brothers would go on record, except one who basically said that whoever talks about the frat or looks into the case gets hurt." There's a minute or two of silence where Nate just stares. "Oh, and there's barely anything about it. The C.P. officers bumbled their way through it, and the local police don't seem any better. It's unbelievable to me."

"Christ," he finally swears.

"Yeah. So now I'm conducting a secret investigation into the original murder at the house and trying to figure out who killed the brother," I sum up. Nate takes a big breath and lets it go in a sigh. Then he laughs. "Why are you laughing?"

"You really don't let anything go, do you?" he asks.

"I can't," I say simply. Nate shakes his head with a grin.

"You're out of your mind, Brooklyn Perce," he says in loving disbelief. I laugh a bit with him. Nate leans back to stretch and then puts his arms on the table in a final sort of way. "Alright I'm in."

"What?"

"Babe, I'm in a frat. I'm sure some of those guys must've heard what happened," he says like it's obvious.

"No. Do *not* say anything to them," I unintentionally snap.

"Why not? They could help!" I groan at my own stupidity. I grab my phone out of my pocket and bring up the screenshots of the anonymous texts, sliding the phone across the table.

"I left out one small detail," I say as Nate takes the phone. His cocky look turns into horror quickly. "They're onto me." Nate's eyes flick up from the phone to meet my gaze.

"Who's 'they'?" I shrug. "Brooklyn, how many of these have you gotten?" he asks in a hushed terrified tone.

"They called me once, and I didn't recognize the voice. I got that text the same night as your frat formal, and I haven't gotten another one since," I tell him. Nate slides the phone back to me.

"They said they want to kill you?" he whispers.

"No, but I think it's safe to say that if I get too close, they'll make sure I don't get closer," I say quietly as people pass by us to enter Rosenburg.

"Who else knows you're doing this?" asks Nate.

"Drew, Kenni, and now you," I say. "This is *strictly* need to know, okay? Don't tell anyone about this."

"Of course. Trust me, I don't want to attend my girlfriend's funeral," he says with a halfhearted laugh. "What are you planning to do next?"

"I'm going to call C.P. and see if I can access their records about the case. They should be public knowledge, so I shouldn't have any problem."

"What about your friend Finn? Didn't you say he might be behind this? Shouldn't you stay away from him until you know for sure that he's not involved?"

"Finn was adopted from an orphanage a few towns over. He didn't know either of his parents, but he somehow knows—or thinks—they were involved in Greek life."

Nate's eyebrows crease. "How would he know that but not who his parents are or where they might be?" he asks.

I shrug. "Freaking beats me. I think Finn's adopted parents scared him into thinking Greek life made his parents abandon him somehow. They probably told it to him when he was little when he found out he was adopted."

Nate snorts. "Great idea. *Always* blame the Greek kids 'cause we're *horrible* people," he scoffs, clearly annoyed.

"I know you guys aren't, but maybe the adopted parents had something against Greek life? I'm not sure, but I have to call the orphanage and ask for his file or whatever they've kept on him." I stop as my thoughts consume me. Nate sighs.

"What do you think about frats? Seriously."

"They're fine, but too often this sort of thing happens. Guys get hurt or they wind up dead. I looked into the Penn State scandal with Drew and it made me nauseous. The guys in fraternities aren't inherently bad. Sometimes, though, there are a few that give the entire community a bad name," I say, choosing my words carefully. Nate doesn't say anything. He just nods along. I relax back in my chair, still thinking about Finn. "The largest problem I'm having with this whole thing is the orphanage is not going to give the records to me because I'm not Finn..." I trail off and raise my eyebrows as an idea comes to mind. Nate looks confused, but then he seems to get the message.

"Brook, there's a reason I didn't do theater in high school," Nate warns slowly.

"You said you wanted to help! This is helping!" I say excitedly. Nate stands up and puts his backpack on. I stand too and put my hands on his sweatshirt, standing on my tiptoes to look him in the eyes. Nate glances reluctantly down at me as my mouth is stretched into the biggest, toothiest smile I've ever made. He raises his eyebrows, and I break my smile into a laugh. Finally, he dramatically groans.

"You're lucky I like you, Perce."

11

"Brooklyn! Need that story from you in a half hour!" Ryker yells to me from across the room. Another Thursday, another shift at the station.

"I'll email it to you in ten!" I shout back out of the door of the editing booth. I quickly make changes and read the story out loud to myself to make sure it makes sense for the anchor. When I hear a knock on the door, I swivel around in my chair.

"Hey Brooklyn," says Lukas. His glasses are on the end of his nose as he looks down at me. "I have a question for you."

"Alright shoot."

"Could you possibly come in tomorrow? Someone canceled on their shift and since you're the newest one around here, you're first to get thrown in the spot," he says. I get my phone to look at my calendar. Other than calling the orphanage, I have nothing to do. I nod at Lukas.

"Yeah I can. What time?" I ask.

"Same as now. Around noon," he says. I give him a thumbs up, and he leaves the editing suite.

I email my story to Ryker and then close out of the audio program I was using to edit soundbites. I Google the phone number of the C.P. office and make sure the editing booth's door is shut before calling it. It rings twice before someone picks up the line.

"Resslar University Campus Police Department, this is Mia, how can I assist you today?" The woman on the other end of the phone speaks so fast that those three sentences sound like one. I clear my throat.

"Hi. My name is Brooklyn. I'm doing a follow-up story about an incident on campus and I was wondering if you might have any information for me about it," I say politely.

"A follow-up story about what?" Mia asks. I swallow hard. If someone is tapping my phone, this is when they'll know what I'm up to.

"Um, the banning of the Sigma Eta Alpha fraternity," I practically whisper. I look over my shoulder out of the window in the door behind me. There's no one there.

"What publication is this for?" asks Mia. She sounds confused.

"Oh, I'm sorry I didn't specify. I work for WRDW," I say. I hear Mia type something into her computer and my heart starts to beat faster.

"One moment please." Mia puts me on hold, so I hear classical music. I put the phone on speaker and put the thing down on the table in front of me, my leg shaking with anxiety.

"Hey." Ryker's voice makes me jump. He pokes his head into the editing booth. "Did you email me the story?"

"Yeah," I say.

"Who are you on the phone with?" he asks, hearing a Vivaldi song come through my phone.

"I'm making a doctor's appointment," I say.

Ryker winces. "Don't get me sick," he teases with a wink.

"I'll try not to," I reassure him as I smile faintly. Ryker shuts the door, and I sigh in relief.

"Ma'am?" Mia says. I put the phone to my ear and take it off of speaker mode.

"Yes?"

"The public only has partial access to the summaries of those records. I could give you everything that's allowed by law, but that would be it," Mia explains. *Something's better than nothing.*

"That would be fine," I say.

"Alright. Would you like them emailed or would you like me to make copies and send them to you?" Mia asks.

"Could I pick up copies on my way by?" I ask her. I don't want any electronic record, lest someone breaks into my laptop again.

"Yes. We close at 5 today."

"Alright thank you so much. I'll come by in fifteen minutes," I say.

"See you then. Good-bye." Mia hangs up on me and I deflate, leaning back in the chair. It makes sense. Since Resslar is a private university, maybe they can decide to release only what they want to release. I just hope what I need is in those summaries.

I call Nate and pack up my bag as the phone is ringing. My boyfriend picks up with a yawn.

"Hello?" he says in a scratchy voice.

"Hey babe," I say cheerily.

"Oh hey! How are you doing?" he asks. "Sorry I'm a bit groggy. I don't have class until four, and I'm taking a nap."

"I'm sorry I woke you up."

"Nah. Don't be. What's up?"

"I called C.P. They said the file about the SHA case is only partially open to the public, so I'm taking every document that the public can have. I'm picking them up on my way home." I then leave the editing booth and wave good-bye to Ryker who's sitting at the desk outside, typing away. He does a salute, and I leave him alone.

The sky today is cloudy and gray. It looks like it might rain at any moment, and I forgot a jacket. I decide it's best to get home as soon as I can, but I need to stop at the C.P. building first.

"Why are the files off limits?" Nate says with a yawn.

"Something legal, I bet. I'll try to figure out how to get the rest of the…" I trail off as I look at the SHA house looming over me.

"Are you passing the house now?" Nate asks.

"How did you know?" I laugh, rounding the corner and heading towards the C.P. office down the street.

"You went quiet all of a sudden. What are you thinking about?" Nate says.

"This entire thing is going to break me," I say with a half-hearted chuckle.

"If you break, I'll put you back together," Nate reassures me.

"Wow, what a line," I say sarcastically. I pass the bus stop on my left and the Biology Building on my right. I get to the end of the street and see the C.P. office on my right. It looks like every other office on this campus: a deteriorating house that was remodeled on the inside. I walk up the stairs to the white house and pray the rickety wooden steps don't collapse underneath my feet. "Hey, I'm going into the C.P. building. I'll see you later, alright?"

"Okay Brook. I love you," Nate says.

"Love you too," I say before hitting the red 'End Call' button.

The inside of the C.P. building looks like a house that was converted into an office. There's a waiting area on my right with seats and a fireplace. In front of me under the stairs is a sign-in desk, and the room on my left looks like it's used for conferences. I can only assume there are offices upstairs. The woman at the front desk is a smaller brunette woman. She looks younger, but the lines on her face clearly indicate she's over 30. The woman looks warily at me.

"Hello. What can I do for you?" I recognize her voice as the one I heard a few minutes ago.

"Hi. I called about the fraternity house paperwork," I tell her cheerily.

"Ah. I think it's all printed. There are about 30 pages front and back." I blink hard. 60 pages of summaries and there are still some C.P. won't let me see. "Let me go check the status of the pages." Mia leaves the desk and goes in a back room. I peer over the desk to look at the computer screen. She closed out the document's file so there goes my plan of sending the rest to myself. I reach for the mouse on the desk, and I'm about to grab it when Mia comes back with a folder.

"Is that it?" I say, collecting myself and then reaching for the folder.

"Yes, these are all of them," she confirms. "I'm surprised WRDW wants to do a story roughly twenty years after the incident."

"I don't question my boss. Not a good idea," I half-heartedly joke, throwing in chuckle to try to sell it. Mia smiles and nods in understanding.

"I hope they're helpful," she says, nodding to the papers.

"Me too. Thanks so much for your help," I reply. I turn around and am about to walk out of the door when I hear a familiar voice.

"Perce!" barks Officer Greenwood. After trying to hold back an angry sigh, I slowly turn on my heel and see him standing on the stairs, leaning his arms on the banister. What's even more frightening than a grown man leering at me from the top of a set of stairs is the look on his face. Greenwood's expression indicates I'm the last person he wanted to see today. He narrows his eyes as he stares at me. "And I thought my day was going well."

"Hello Officer Greenwood," I sweetly chirp, putting the folder at my side and giving him a big smile. "How are you?"

"I'm fine. The better question is why are you here?" he sneers, coming down the stairs. Greenwood comes to stand in front of me and crosses his arms. I'm looking at him with big dewy eyes and the smuggest smile on my face. I'm suddenly aware of how much bigger he is than me. "What are you up to?" I shake my head and raise an eyebrow.

"Nothing Officer. I was just getting some documents for a story for WRDW that I have to write," I say in the most innocent voice I possibly can.

Greenwood's brows come together as he searches my face. "Right," he says slowly. He bites his tongue and turns around to look at the receptionist. "Mia, what did you give her?" Mia looks at me, and I widen my eyes in fright. Mia looks back at Greenwood and shrugs.

"She's writing a story about the number of sexual assault incidents on campus. She needed the numbers," Mia says calmly, going back to whatever she was typing. Greenwood turns back to me. I smile smugly at him. He looks down at the 30 sheets of paper in my hand.

"So those must be all summaries then since we don't give out any specific information to the public. Unless you filed a Freedom of Information Act to get everything which I highly doubt you did," summarizes Greenwood. I gulp and keep looking into the cop's eyes. *Well at least my guess about releasing the summaries was correct.* Greenwood smirks and I start to back up. "You know how much trouble you can get into for lying to an officer?" I decide it's best to save the snappy remarks for Taylor. I keep my mouth shut as Greenwood keeps getting closer, and I keep walking backwards.

"I'm just trying to write a story, Sir," I assure him.

Greenwood nods. "Right." He gives me one last hard look and then jerks towards the door with his chin. "Go." I stumble backwards and run out of the C.P. office.

❈ ❈ ❈

"Alright let's see what we have." I'm sitting on the floor of my room in between the two beds. Nate is sitting on the floor with me, his back leaning against the leg of my bed. Drew is sitting on her mattress, her legs lazily dangling. It's nine o'clock at night on a Thursday, and we're sitting in my room going through the C.P. documents. I make a mental note to get my priorities straightened out.

123

"What are we looking for?" asks Nate as I hand him a stack of papers.

"I think it's pretty clear," Drew says sarcastically as she flips through her papers. "Look out for any reports of a dead guy, and we should be set." Nate rolls his eyes and takes the highlighter I'm giving to him.

"What the hell did they not release to the public? These summaries seem thorough," Nate asks, starting to read page one.

"I have no idea. I figure if there's information that was left out of these, we try to fill in the blanks ourselves. In the meantime, tell me if you find something crucial, and I'll write it down," I instruct.

We sit there for two hours putting the reports in chronological order. By the time we're done, Nate and I are sitting on my bed and Drew is standing on her desk looking down at our new paper carpet. The entire floor is covered in C.P. reports with different colored highlighter marks on them. It's overwhelming to look at so much evidence at once. Drew finally hops onto her desk chair and looks down at the mess.

"How is it eleven?" she yawns, looking at the clock on our microwave.

"*That's* what you're thinking about?" Nate asks. "Brook, how are we going to go through all of this?" I shake my head.

"Let's just go through and read the reports in order. Maybe that'll tell us something," I suggest. Since she has the smallest feet, my roommate hops onto the ground and looks at the first sheet by the head of my bed.

"This one is about improper conduct reported at the house. Actually, the first couple are about that," Drew says as she scans the documents.

"What kind of stuff?" Nate prods, craning his neck to see the page she's looking at.

"Mostly hazing related incidents. There are reports of people going to health services because of the beatings they took during initiation," Drew explains, wincing as she reads it. She gets to the middle of the room and keeps going as I type down notes. "Alright, these are a bit more damning."

"How so?" I ask, my fingers ready to type.

"The chapter at Resslar was reported to, like, the head Sigma Eta Alpha organization in New York City. And then officials from there did a sweep of the house and found the brothers were dealing drugs out of it," summarizes Drew.

"How is drug dealing related to Finn's parents?" Nate wonders aloud. I shrug in response.

"Let me keep reading," Drew scolds, shutting up Nate. She scans the next few rows of papers. "Okay, so it seems like they were caught dealing in the middle of March in 1997. The hazing stuff seems like it had been going on for a while before any brother actually reported it. The first guy came forward in what seems like the second-to-last week in February of that year. They were going to be given until the end of March by the university to pack up and leave. The university scheduled a trial for the frat at the end of March. But then..." Drew trails off.

Nate raises his eyebrows. "Then what?" he pushes.

Drew looks angrily at Nate. "You *really* don't want me to read, do you?" she huffs. She looks at me. "Can you control your boyfriend please?"

"No promises," I tell her. Nate gives me a smile and nudges me with his shoulder.

Drew sticks her tongue out like she's pretending to vomit and then continues, "Alright, to finish my sentence, the frat was told to get out by the end of March. They put extra cops around the house and removed the boys who were causing the most problems. But then they threw one last party and that morning at three, someone called reporting a death at the house." The room is silent as we all let that sink in. "The frat was immediately disbanded."

"Jesus Christ," breathes Nate.

"This doesn't name a suspect," Drew points out.

"They're saying it's his girlfriend. All of the online reports I read said that anyway," I fill in. Nate shakes his head and reads off of a paper sitting near him.

"Yeah, but the guy died of blunt force trauma and had marks on his neck 'indicating strangulation.' What girl do you know is strong enough to strangle a guy twice her size *and* beat the hell out of him?" Nate asks. "Not that girls are physically weak," he quickly says after a pointed look from Drew. "I'm just saying, he's stated as being six-foot-one and 200 pounds. Hitting a guy that big over and over would be tough. And strangling someone takes sustained force against someone who's probably struggling. And if the person who's struggling is a dude, how hard do you have to squeeze to choke him?"

"You seem like you know a lot about this," I say, somewhat surprised.

Nate just shrugs. "I watch movies, and I have two brothers. I figure that's what it takes."

"So, if none of the brothers had it out for him and the girlfriend didn't have the force to do it, then who did?" asks Drew.

"And *that* right there is the question," I concede.

12

The next day, I'm back at the WRDW office trying to write a story for the 5 o'clock news, but I can't concentrate. My mind can't focus on anything other than the information I learned last night. How did the frat not get shut down sooner? And how were they allowed to throw one final party where everything went to hell? Did *no one* here care about what was going on with the brothers?

The cursor on the screen blinks expectantly, just waiting for the order from my fingers to type letters onto the screen. I let out an exasperated groan and put my head in my hands. I hate writer's block, especially when my brain isn't in the creative mood. As I silently wish for someone to save me, I hear the soft *click* of the door behind me.

"Hey Brooklyn." Ryker's voice makes me jump. I turn around in my swivel chair. "Peter wants to see you." My stomach flips.

"Um, alright." I get up out of my chair. "Did he tell you what for?"

"No, but I'm sure you'll be fine," reassures Ryker. I follow him up the stairs to Peter's opulent office. With every step, I become more nervous. *I don't think I did anything wrong...Did I?* Ryker knocks on Peter's door and then opens it slowly.

"Peter?" Ryker offers. Peter turns away from his computer and nods, giving Ryker a smile.

"Yes, Brooklyn, come in please," he says in his cold tone. I gulp and sit down in the same chair I sat in when I was interviewed. My leg shakes nervously out of Peter's view. Ryker goes to leave, but Peter shakes his head. "No Ryker. I would like you to stay." Peter gestures to the seat on my left, and Ryker looks confused, but he sits down anyway. Peter shuts his laptop and folds his hands on his desk.

"Why do you want me to stay?" Ryker asks politely.

"You're her supervisor. I want you to be here for this," Peter answers. *Oh no.* My leg shakes harder. "Brooklyn, I received an interesting call from a C.P. officer this morning. He said his name was Roger Greenwood." I swallow hard. "Officer Greenwood said you were in the C.P. office the other day asking for files for a story for WRDW." *That freaking bastard.* Ryker's eyes slide over to me then back to Peter. "Now, I thought that was funny since you're not supposed to go out and report about stories for the station without clearance from Ryker and myself. I had to lie to the officer to save face."

"Sir, I can explain," I say hurriedly, but Peter holds up a hand to stop me.

"Now, Officer Greenwood said he didn't know exactly what the files contained, but he did say that you were very intent on leaving the building." There's silence. "Care to explain?" I try to stop my leg from shaking but it's no use.

"I... I was getting C.P. records for a side project I've been working on," I say, choosing every word I say with intense care.

"So you lied to the officer to seem legitimate?" Peter fills in.

"I just thought if I gave them a name, they would be more likely to release the records," I reason. Peter shakes his head.

"You're not allowed to do that whatsoever," he says. I nod, not making eye contact with him. "That's strictly against the policy of the station. You can't lie to people to get what you want, *especially* to an officer."

"I understand, and I'm so sorry Peter," I apologize, finally looking at him.

Peter shakes his head. He strokes his clean chin, clearly in thought. "Look, you're one of the best writers we have in the newsroom. Ryker tells me you're a hard worker, very diligent and punctual. For that reason, I'm not going to fire you." I sigh quietly. "But I don't want to *ever* hear that you're using our station as a cover for some side project. Understand?"

"Yes, Sir. I completely understand," I hurriedly say, swallowing and nodding. "It won't happen again. I promise."

"Alright." Peter bites his lip and leans back in his chair. "If you don't mind me asking, what were the files you were trying to access?" My brain goes into panic mode. I can't tell Peter what I'm doing, but I already lied to him once. Ryker looks at me, his leg shaking too.

"Well, my boyfriend is in a fraternity, and he was telling me about the Sigma Eta Alpha house," I explain slowly. Ryker raises his eyebrows and looks at Peter with wide eyes. Peter sticks his tongue in his cheek, his eyebrows raised as well.

"Ryker, would you mind leaving us alone?" Peter requests after a second. Ryker looks at me with concern and then nods.

"Sure," he says simply. Ryker gets up and after looking over his shoulder, opens the door and leaves, shutting it behind him.

Peter leans forward. "Why are you looking into that house?" Peter questions sternly. I shake my head and try to find a reason. "Brooklyn, answer me."

"I can't give you an answer other than morbid curiosity," I say, shrugging my shoulders with an innocent smile.

Peter pinches the bridge of his nose with his ring finger and thumb. "Have you figured out what happened to the journalists who looked into that story?" Peter asks after a second.

"Yeah, I found two stories about—"

"No, no, no, I mean have you *heard* what happened to them?" Peter says in a quiet voice. His tone indicates he thinks we're being watched. I shake my head. "It happened the fifth year I was here. We did little coverage of the entire ordeal because it was so dangerous to send reporters to the scene. Since SHA is a national fraternity, the whole thing made headlines which other chapters at other schools have tried to erase from history. That's probably why you can't find much on it. Anyway, reporters came from everywhere, not just New York state, to try to figure out who killed the fraternity brother. Things seemed to be going well. People were publishing things, and it seemed like the public was really into the story. Murders always seem to grab people's attention. It's sick but it's true. But then people started to go missing." Peter shakes his head, looking past my face at the wall behind me. "And entire stories were redacted. And then a journalist was found dead in front of the house."

"I read that story," I whisper, my lips barely moving.

"The police got involved when C.P. failed, but even they couldn't find anything leading back to who killed the men. A lot of papers stopped covering the story, dropped it all together. We never sent a reporter close to the issue. We only circled the problem, and we made sure that the guy we sent was equipped with self-defense tools. Thank God no one from this station was hurt, but it was a scary time. After the Academic Board trial where they banned the fraternity, campus tried to go back to normal. The police and C.P. blamed it on the brother's girlfriend, closed the case, and no one ever questioned what happened to the house. But here you are, trying to figure out what about a hundred journalists were unable to uncover." I give a little apologetic smile. Peter leans back in his chair. He looks like he's thinking about something. "I'll tell you what," he continues after a second or two of silence. "I can't think of a better reporter to reopen the case." I look at him hopefully. "Brooklyn, if you actually figure out what happened to that fraternity, you can write an entire *New York Times*-style exposé about it. You'll get an entire staff and have them help you write it, the whole thing. You're a smart kid, and I trust you wouldn't take on anything you thought you couldn't handle."

"Really?" I hesitate, trying to hold back my disbelief.

Peter nods. "And since you will be writing a story for us, you have my permission to worked under the title of WRDW reporter. But you have to promise me that you'll be careful about it. If you need my help, call the station, you know I'm always here. Ryker as well. Be smart, be safe, and don't make a decision you might regret."

"Thank you so much, Sir," I say breathlessly. Peter gives me a tight smile and nods, dismissing me.

"Stay safe, Brooklyn," he says. I turn around and open the door of the office. I jump back a bit when I find Ryker still standing in the hallway. He quickly looks up from his phone.

"Are you guys all good?" he asks urgently, standing up from his leaning position against the wall.

"Yeah," I say.

Ryker passes by me and enters Peter's office. "I've got a meeting with him now. I'll see you downstairs," he says. When I turn to go, I feel Ryker grab my wrist. He spins me around so I can look at him. I have half a mind to rip my arm out of his grasp, but he seems jarred. His eyes remind me of a panther's the way they stare intently at me. "By the way, that house? Don't go near it. It's trouble."

"Calm down, *Dad*. I haven't gotten in trouble yet," I tell him jokingly. He scoffs, nose twitching. Ryker lets me go, and I calmly walk away from him as he stares at my back.

I go downstairs and sit back in front of the computer screen, my fingers typing at a slower pace than my brain is thinking.

"You're freaking kidding me," Nate says incredulously as I tell him what happened at the radio station.

I shake my head and stop pacing in front of him. "I thought he was going to fire me. He had Ryker come in and everything," I say. Nate looks confused. "Ryker is my boss at the station. He's a senior."

"Gotcha." Nate leans back in his chair and then puts his forearms on the table in front of him. I sit down next to him and cross my arms. We both stare at my phone which is sitting on the tabletop between us. "We're seriously going to do this?" I wordlessly nod. "What if they ask for his Social Security number? Or they ask me some personal question that I don't know the answer to?" I open up the page of notes that I was taking the other day.

"I have Finn's date of birth, his address, the names of his adopted parents, and his high school," I rattle off.

"Does he know you're doing this?" Nate asks.

I shake my head and chew on my thumb nail. "He doesn't even want to *see* the records. He made that pretty clear," I say, remembering the conversation I had with Finn in his dorm room.

"Brooklyn, you got lucky once today with your boss actually *backing* this project. I'm not comfortable pushing that luck," Nate tells me.

"What's the worst thing that could happen?" I ask him.

"They call the cops on me for identity fraud!" Nate exclaims. I bite my lip.

"Okay, good point," I agree. Nate puts his head in his hands then looks at the expectant phone through his fingers. I put my hand on his shoulder and rub it.

I've never seen him this vulnerable before and it's a bit nerve-wracking. "Nate, I know this is a huge thing to ask you to do and if you don't want to do it now, I totally understand." Nate looks at me and searches my face. "I should've never dragged you into this anyway."

"No. No, I pushed you to tell me about it that day when you came into my room and that was wrong of me to do." He looks at me and puts his hand on my cheek. "I'm so proud of your bravery and that you can do shit like this because I clearly lack the guts." Nate looks at the phone, takes a deep breath, then grabs it. "Alright, what's the number?" I tell Nate the phone number of the orphanage and then have him put the call on speaker. The phone rings and rings. I don't think anyone is going to pick up, but then a friendly female voice rings through the room.

"Lakewood Orphanage," she greets. I see Nate scramble for a second, but then he collects himself.

"Hi, my name is Finnigan Larson. I was hoping to get a copy of my biological parents' most recent medical records. I had to visit the health center on campus and the doctors wanted to know if I had a family history of any allergies to medication," Nate says in a level voice. He looks at me with wide eyes, and I see him swallow hard. He's nervous and scared, and I can't blame him.

"What's your date of birth?" the receptionist asks.

"Eighteen," rushes Nate in a trembling voice. He realizes his misstep. "Oh sorry, um, March 20th, 1997." We hear typing on the other end.

"Alright you are 18, so you do have the right to ask for your records without your parent's approval," the receptionist says like she's talking to herself. I see Nate's leg shaking under the table. The free hand he has on the table is in a fist. I can tell his fingertips are digging into his palm. He *hates* doing this. Part of me wants to grab the phone from him, hang up and forget this ever happened.

"Mr. Larson, do you have your Social Security number with you?" As soon as she says it, Nate puts his head down on the table. My stomach drops. There's a second of silence. Nate picks his head up and runs a hand through his hair.

"Um, I didn't know I would have to have that on hand," he says. "Is there another piece of information I could give you?"

"I mean, that's a primary form of identification to verify that you are who you say you are," says the receptionist. Nate looks over at me with the expression of someone who's given up on life. There's no way that we can make up a Social Security number. We're screwed. Nate closes his eyes and sighs, his bottom lip tight with stress.

"Is there any way you can overlook that? The doctors on campus can't prescribe me anything without knowing my medical history. I mean, I wouldn't be asking for the records if I didn't absolutely need them," Nate slightly presses.

"Could you call your adopted family and ask them for the documents? They should have them at home," the receptionist suggests.

"I did and they said they misplaced them. They said I should call you guys," Nate lies. The receptionist sighs. I can feel my heart beating in my throat. Nate quickly unclenches his fist and grabs my hand with his.

"Alright Mr. Larson, I will send you the documents even though I'm not supposed to without a social security number. Just have it next time, okay?" Nate's body collapses with relief on the table in front of him. He doesn't say anything for a bit as he lies there stunned. "Mr. Larson?"

"Yes, I'll remember for next time. Thank you so much," Nate says faintly.

"I'll email them to you so you can show them to your physician, and they'll print them," says the receptionist. "Can I get an email?" I push a piece of paper in front of him with the fake email address I made.

"It's finnlar3@gmail.com," he says in a stronger voice as he reads off of the page. I whack Nate on the arm and give him a thumbs up.

"Okay, I just sent them. Call us back if you need anything else, but please have identification on you," the receptionist advises.

"Will do. Thanks so much," Nate says.

"Good-bye." She hangs up the phone, and Nate taps the 'End Call' button, dropping my phone on the table after doing so.

Nate and I just stare at my phone in disbelief. He puts his head down on the table and sighs.

"I love you," I whisper to Nate, breaking the silence.

"Yeah. I love you too," Nate says weakly, the statement muffled by the tabletop.

13

"What a lucky bitch you are," Drew says to me at breakfast the next morning when I tell her what happened the other night.

"I thought I was going to pass out," I say truthfully.

"How did Nate do it?" she asks. I shrug and spear another cube of watermelon with my fork.

"He just did it. He said he didn't act in high school, but that repressed gene came out last night," I tell her.

Drew laughs. "Yeah, what else did you two do last night?" she asks. "I haven't seen you until you left to make the call at, like, five."

"We got some food, went back to his room, watched a movie, went up to the roof of Cypress to watch the stars, and made out a lot," I casually recap. Drew raises an eyebrow. "No, I didn't sleep with him if that was the answer you wanted." I laugh a bit when she wilts.

"Alright," she says like I let her down. "The guy deserved it though."

"Deserved it or not, didn't happen."

She sits back in her chair. "So, when are we gonna have a look at those documents?" she asks.

"What documents?" Finn walks up to our table, a heaping plate of eggs and bacon in his hands. He sits down next to me and takes a sip of his water.

Unraveling

"For that orphanage story I told you I was working on," I say, not without a confused glance from Drew. "I got some numbers from the state about adoption rates and stuff like that. It's interesting."

"Sounds like it," says Finn. "So you've dropped the frat thing?" Drew coughs, taken aback by his comment. I look over at him.

"Yeah," I say after a second, moving the fruit on my plate around.

Finn snorts, a little annoyed smile on his face. "You're lying. Why the hell can't you let this go?" Finn groans.

"Why do you want to talk about this at ten in the morning on a Saturday?" I shoot back.

"I figure I should stop this crazy train as soon as I can before you get yourself killed," says Finn.

"How do you know that could happen?" I ask him.

"Because I'm not an idiot! Look at the facts, Brook. Everyone who gets involved with this disappears or dies."

"Where'd you learn that from?"

"You just hear things. That case defined the campus for the next few years. If anyone doesn't know about it, they're an idiot," Finn says. I give Drew a pointed look that she doesn't return. "Plus, don't you forget I was *born and raised* up here."

"Finn, you're sounding mighty suspicious right now," I say honestly.

"Oh my *God,* you think I'm involved with this?" he exclaims.

"You and Greenwood seem pretty freaking intent on keeping me away from the house!" I shout.

"Who is Greenwood?" Finn practically shrieks.

"He's the C.P. officer who's trying to stop me from figuring this whole thing out."

Finn puts his head in his hands and groans. "Brooklyn, do you realize how insane you sound?" Finn just stares at me with his mouth half open. "You sound batshit crazy. The case is dead for a *reason.*"

"Why don't you want me investigating it?" I snap. "Why?"

"Because you could *die!*" Finn fully yells. People eating around us are staring now, and it's making me uncomfortable. Finn seems to have realized his outburst. He leans back in his chair and crosses his arms, taking measured breaths in and out through his nose.

"I'm not going to die, Finn," I say in a forced calm voice.

"Look, I was wrong to yell at you, and I'm sorry. But Brooklyn, there's a reason no one has looked into this thing. You're one of my best friends, and I don't want to see you hurt," Finn explains.

"That was the sweetest thing I think you've ever said," Drew chimes in. Finn slides his eyes across the table to look at my roommate. They make eye contact and smile at each other.

"How do you know about people dying?" I repeat.

"There were a few frat guys sitting behind me in Newsworthy the other day. They were talking about making initiates spend the night in the empty SHA house. The brothers wanted to scare the shit out of the initiates on purpose," Finn explains.

"Nice," Drew scoffs.

"Anyway, they were throwing that idea around when one of the brothers was like, 'Hey maybe we shouldn't do that because it's trespassing, and we

140

might get killed.' But the idiots put the idea on the list of initiation activities anyway," Finn finishes. "I hope Nate isn't as big of a dick as those guys are."

"Nate's amazing," I reassure Finn.

"He's a nice guy, Finn," Drew confirms.

Finn nods and eats his eggs. "What frat is he in?"

"Delta Rho," I say.

"A buddy of mine is in that frat," Finn remarks.

"It's a big pledge class from what I hear," I say, trying to keep the conversation light. Finn nods and keeps eating. I can tell he's embarrassed by flat out yelling at me, but I know that yelling comes from a place of concern.

"Seriously, I'm sorry for…all that," Finn says genuinely.

"It's okay. Sorry for accusing you." He shrugs.

"It's actually kind of flattering. Not every day you get accused of knowing about one of the greatest unsolved mysteries in Central New York." The two of us share a smile of understanding.

※ ※ ※

Knock knock.

"Who is it?" I yell, getting off of my bed and putting my math homework down. After I look through the peephole to ensure it's not anyone less than friendly, I open the door to my beautiful boyfriend. Nate gives me a smile and bends down to kiss me.

"Hey. Mind if I come in?" he asks.

"Yeah sure." Nate walks in and shuts the door behind him. I lock it quickly. He sighs. "Still paranoid?" I nod and move my homework so he can lie on the bed.

"What's going on?"

"I was bored, so I wanted to see what you were up to."

"I'm doing math homework."

"Glamorous. Hey, do you want to come to another party with me tonight? You can bring Drew or Kenni if you want," Nate offers. When I look hesitant, Nate shakes his head. "It won't be like last time, I promise."

"I mean, if I get to actually spend time with you, I'll go," I say.

Nate smiles. "You will! I won't be networking this time. The brothers who met you really like you," Nate says.

"Seriously? To tell you the truth, I've forgotten their names already," I say with a little laugh.

Nate stands up and tucks my hair behind my ear. "Don't worry about it. Worry about your friend who supposedly wants to kill you," jokes Nate.

I snort and shake my head. "You laugh, but I mentioned the fraternity at breakfast this morning and Finn went nuts," I say.

"Did you say anything about calling the orphanage?" Nate asks, his tone going from flirtatious to scared in a second.

"No, but when I said I was still looking into the frat, he freaked out at me," I explain. Nate groans, hopping onto his feet and leaning against my mattress.

"I still feel bad for impersonating him," Nate says softly. "Do you have the documents though?"

I nod. "Yeah. Thank God I printed them out because they were somehow deleted from the fake email's inbox." Nate's eyes grow, and I give him a tight smile.

"Shit," he swears. "Well, this is exactly why we need a party. It'll distract us from the person trying to get you."

"Will this party end in another make out session on the top of Cypress?" I ask him with an eyebrow raised.

He looks to the ceiling like he's thinking about it. "Only if you want it to," Nate purrs softly, kissing me briefly.

"Alright." I give him one last kiss. "Text me the time you want to leave. See you later." Nate walks away from me and out of the door. When the door slams, I sit at my desk and pick my math papers back up.

Bing. Bing. Bing.

My phone rings with an unknown number. I pick up my phone, my hands shaking. I carefully put the phone to my ear and don't say anything at first. All I hear is heavy breathing until I finally say something.

"Who is this?" I demand in the strongest voice I can. There's no response. "Who are you?" I ask again.

"Drop this case Brooklyn," demands an unknown man's voice.

"No," I say.

"You won't get many more warnings. Drop this." Then the dial tone clicks, and I sit in my room in complete silence.

14

Finishing my math homework was not easy after that call. The silence of my room felt like a prolonged jump scare. Every minute that went by was dragged out to an excruciating length. I was half expecting Drew to come home, but she never did. That anticipation made it even worse. I thankfully make it through the evening without going too stir crazy and when 11 p.m. hits, Nate and I start off towards the Delta Rho house hand-in-hand.

"Drew decided not to come?" Nate asks.

"She's probably hanging out with this kid from her class named Dex. She might stop by later, but I doubt it," I explain.

"Gotcha."

"So, who's gonna be here?" I ask.

"I think most if not all of my brothers and girls of course," Nate says.

The Delta Rho house can be heard once we turn the corner of the street it's on. Muffled music and joyful shouting become louder and louder as we get closer. I can see the brothers have set up colored lights inside and they change in rhythm to the thumping bass. Nate holds the door open for me as I go inside, and the smell of weed makes its way into my nose.

"Let's go out outside!" Nate yells over the deafening house music. I give him a thumbs up, and we push our way to the kitchen where the red-headed Oliver is serving drinks.

"Hey Nate! Hi Brooklyn!" greets Oliver cheerfully.

"Hey Ollie. Give me something," Nate requests. Oliver dumps the contents of a few different bottles into one red cup and hands it to Nate. "Thanks man."

"And for you?" asks Oliver.

"A beer is fine," I say.

"Hey Nate!" yells a new voice. A brown-haired boy who I estimate to be a Junior is pushing through the crowd towards us. A white t-shirt and brown khakis are draped on his skinny but muscular frame. It's all topped off by a baseball cap with the Pittsburgh Steelers logo on it. Nate's face breaks into a smile and he gives the newcomer a hug.

"Hey James! How are you doing, bud?" Nate asks. Oliver hands me the beer and I smile to thank him.

"Doing well! Hey, want to go outside?" James suggests.

"Sure." The three of us go into the backyard of the frat house. The grass is dotted with half-smoked blunts, Natural Light beer cans, and red cups from past games of Pong. We pull up lawn chairs and put them in a circle far enough away from the four guys who are smoking a bowl over by the garage. James sits down and looks at me.

"I'm James Earl, by the way," he says, offering his hand.

I take it and shake. "Brooklyn Perce," I say.

James's face looks confused but turns back to a smile. "*You're* Brooklyn?" he repeats incredulously.

I shrug and take a drink. "In the flesh," I say.

James looks at Nate. "Damn, how did you manage to get a girl like her?" James laughs.

Nate looks at me and smiles. "To tell you the truth, I don't know," he replies. Nate takes my hand and squeezes, looking lovingly at me.

"What's your major?" James asks me.

"Broadcast journalism," I answer.

"Nice. I do political science," says James.

"James is my big," Nate tells me. "Best big there is."

"Aw, shut up," James says, taking a drink out of his cup. When he removes the cup from his lips, he looks like he just tasted something bitter. "Don't ever mix tequila and jack and drink it straight," he advises.

"That sounds horrible," I say. "What year are you, James?"

"Junior," says James. "You're a freshman, right?"

"Yep," I say.

"She works at WRDW," says Nate.

James raises his eyebrows. "Oh, do you know Lukas?" asks James. I nod. "Yeah he's one of my best friends."

"No kidding! I love Lukas," I say.

James shakes his head. "You don't have to pretend to like him. He can be an asshole at times…Well, actually *a lot* of times, but he's great otherwise," says James. "So, what do you report on?"

"Mostly local news, but I'm trying to work on a side project right now." I see Nate shoot me a look that I don't return. My face remains calm.

"What's your side project?" James asks. I take a drink and shrug.

"That's just it. I need to find one. I don't have a good lead on a story yet," I say like it's the darndest thing in the world.

"You want a lead? How about sniffing out the inevitable corruption inside Rosenburg and writing about that?" A familiar voice has joined the conversation. Brendon walks up beside James.

James turns around and smiles. "Hey Brendon. Always in such a chipper mood," James mutters, turning back to us and scoffing.

"There's always a corruption story somewhere. You just have to find it," Brendon advises, sitting down on the grass which is no doubt soaked with beer. Brendon's nose wrinkles. "God, what is that smell?"

"Oh, Greg and some other guys are smoking weed over there," James says. He raises his hand and waves hello to the four boys by the garage. One of them manages to raise his hand up to his shoulder and lazily wave hello. James turns back to us. "Don't do drugs, kids." The four of us laugh and sip our drinks.

"So, you wanted a story?" Brendon asks me, his glasses falling off of his nose.

"If you have one, I'm all ears," I say. Brendon looks at Nate and his lips become a line in his face.

"Ask your boyfriend over there. I'm sure his dad's full of secrets," Brendon casually jabs. James raises his eyebrows, sensing trouble.

"C'mon man, really?" Nate says, exasperated.

Brendon rolls his eyes. "It's pretty obvious your father is a tycoon, Stevenson. The question is if all of your daddy's current dealings are still legal," Brendon smirks, his eyes fixed on Nate.

"Shut up," Nate snarls. I notice how his leg starts to bounce like it did when we were calling the orphanage. His unoccupied hand is subtly curling into a fist.

Brendon looks at me and puts his hands up in surrender. "All I'm saying is your boyfriend has got some skeletons in his closet," Brendon sighs. I glance at Nate whose eyes flick from his brother to me as he chews on the inside of his cheek. Nate finally takes a big swig of his drink and breaks into a forced smile.

"I don't know why you're being such a tool. I'm your brother," Nate says with a short laugh that sounds more like a bark.

"Even family members have secrets," says Brendon calmly. Nate furiously looks across the circle to Brendon who has a level look on his face. "You out of everyone should know that."

Nate springs up out of his chair, downs the rest of his drink, then looks down at me. "Brooklyn, we're leaving," Nate says declaratively.

"We just got here," I say, mildly scared at what's going on.

"Yeah, and we're clearly not wanted. Now let's go," Nate snaps forcefully with urgency.

"Don't refuse an order from Stevenson, Brooklyn," Brendon mockingly reminds me. Nate makes a move for Brendon, but I stand up and get in between them. I look sternly at my boyfriend. He's turned into this skittish and defensive creature that I don't recognize. I stare into his eyes, hoping he receives my silent message to calm himself down. Nate looks at me, then at Brendon, then back at me. He finally drops his tough guy act and backs up a few steps but doesn't break eye contact with Brendon. James stands up and taps Nate on the shoulder.

"C'mon man, let's talk," James says to him softly. Nate gets up without saying a word and follows James as they walk towards the side of the house.

I watch them walk away then look at Brendon who keeps drinking his beer as though nothing happened. "What the hell was that about?" I exclaim.

Brendon rolls his eyes. "Your boyfriend isn't innocent. I told you that the last time we talked. You should've listened to me," Brendon chides. I make a sound of disgust and cross my legs, sipping my beer that tastes like muddy water.

"At least he didn't murder anyone," I say in a quiet voice.

"At least he didn't *what?*" Brendon asks, practically cutting me off. I realize what I just said and try to take back my words, but my scramble makes Brendon realize what I'm talking about. "Did you just find out about the SHA house?" I nod and Brendon nods along with me. "Yeah, it was awful. There are new state-wide policies now that you can't haze. Or maybe the policies are that you *can* haze, just not so it physically hurts anyone, I'm not sure."

"How did you find out about the house?" I ask him.

"I walked past it enough times and I asked my big about it. He just told me the basics, and I didn't question it." I look over at Nate who's talking to James and looking back at Brendon vengefully. When Nate looks at me, he grimaces like he knows how embarrassing his outburst was. My head turns to look at Brendon who's just staring at me innocently.

"Better go calm down your Pit Bull," he mutters loud enough so I can hear.

"Just shut up," I retort. I walk over to Nate and put my hand on his shoulder. He still seems rattled by Brendon's comment.

"I'll let you two go if you want," James says kindly.

Nate looks down at me and softly smiles. "Yeah what do you think? I'm not in the mood to party anymore," Nate says.

"I need to do work anyway," I agree with a little eyebrow raise, so he knows what I mean.

Nate nods and shakes James' hand. "Thanks for understanding, man. Kick Brendon's ass for me," Nate requests.

"Not while I'm drunk," James says, toasting his red cup in the air. "Later dude." He claps Nate on the back and starts to walk back towards the house, leaving Brendon alone outside. Nate takes me by the hand, and we start to walk up the driveway back towards the street. As we get farther away from the house, Nate becomes more and more upset.

"You alright?" I ask him.

"No," snaps Nate immediately. "He's an asshole, talking about my dad as if he knows anything."

"Just breathe, it'll be okay." Nate rounds on me and I can almost see the steam coming out of his ears. "What was Brendon talking about?" I ask gently. Nate shakes his head violently and keeps walking.

"I can't tell you. You'd never trust me again," Nate murmurs.

"What? Nate, I trusted you with the story, you can't trust me with this?" I gently point out. Nate stays quiet and keeps shaking his head and scoffing.

Finally, I grab his wrist out of exasperation and spin him around so he's a few feet away from me.

"What?" he asks through his teeth.

"What was Brendon talking about?" I say tightly.

Nate sighs. "Brooklyn, you need to learn when to let something go," Nate relents, tucking a piece of hair behind my ear in defeat. I back up so he can't touch me. "What's wrong with you?"

"What's wrong with *me*?" I repeat incredulously. "Nate, you turned into a monster back there."

"I wouldn't call me a monster," Nate says.

"You weren't the one watching that little interaction." Nate looks like I've caught him in a lie. "What's wrong, Nate? Really." Nate runs his hands through his hair and lets out a big breath of air. He seems so ready for this night to be over that I feel somewhat bad for pressuring him into giving me an answer. Nate sits down on the lawn to our left and puts his head in his hands. I sit down next to him and just rest my head on his shoulder until he looks back up at the street.

"My dad was and is the only source of income for our family. He worked at this investment corporation when I was little. I was about five when the cops arrested him because he was stealing from his clients." I put my hands over my mouth. Nate nods and looks at the road, still not able to look at me. "He was tried, found guilty, then put in prison for a couple years. Eventually, my mom came up with the money to pay his bail. Ironically, some of that bail money was stolen from my dad's investors." Nate scoffs and shakes his head. "When my dad got out of jail, he was a changed man. He got a new job, and now he's back at a firm in the city. And the reason why Brendon is up my ass about it is because one of

Brendon's relatives lost money to my father." Nate laughs to himself. "Funny how the world works, right?" It's silent for a couple minutes. The few cars on the road pass us by and a pack of tipsy girls carefully teeters on the sidewalk across the street. I laugh a little bit and hug his bicep.

"I think I can keep that under wraps," I quietly assure him, looking into his beautiful eyes. Nate snorts and smiles down at me. "You're not your father, Nate. You're honest and kind."

"You don't know me well enough to say that," Nate says softly.

"Yeah I do. I know you wouldn't hurt a soul. Even when a soul tries to provoke you when they're half drunk," I tease. After softly scoffing, Nate pushes my hair back from my face and stares into my eyes. "You aren't your father, you aren't a horrible person, and you sure as hell aren't like that scumbag back at the house." He looks pitifully into my eyes.

"I love you," Nate says before kissing me. He puts his hand behind my neck, and I turn my body towards him, putting a hand on his chest. We start to make out right there on some stranger's front lawn, the two of us completely sober. I don't remember how long I was sitting, but I do remember that when we stopped, my lips hurt.

"Ow-OW! Get it, Stevenson!" yells a frat brother from the porch of another frat house. Nate groans, gives the guy the finger, and rests his head on my shoulder as I start to laugh.

"I can never get any privacy," jokes Nate, turning to look at the frat house three doors down. When he waves at them, they wave back.

"That's what you get for being a star," I quip. I kiss him again and stand, offering him my hand so he can get up too. "C'mon Stevenson. Let's go home."

15

I wake up to the sound of my phone ringing.

My hand tries to grab it from the windowsill, but my fingers don't find the ringing phone. They don't even find the windowsill.

That's when I realize that I'm not in my bed.

I sit bolt upright and look around at Nate's dorm room. When I try to run a hand through my hair, I find that it's tangled. When I look to my left, I see my boyfriend lying there with his shirtless back facing me. From somewhere in the room, my phone keeps incessantly ringing.

Where is the damn thing?

I look around for it and see it near my jeans on the floor next to the bed. The phone stops for two seconds, then rings again. I carefully get out of bed and throw on a sweatshirt of Nate's that I found on the floor. The soft inside feels nice on my bare chest. I pick up the phone and put it to my ear.

"Where the hell are you? It's almost eleven! Have you been kidnapped?" Drew rushes frantically before I can get a word out.

"No, Crazy! I'm in Nate's dorm." I hear Drew suck in a breath of air.

"Oh *shit*! I'm *so* sorry. I just wanted to make sure you weren't taken or something. I'll see you later." With that, my roommate hangs up on me. I groan and

154

walk back to Nate's bed, going around the other side so I can see his face. He's sleeping soundly as I crouch down next to him and clear his hair out of his face. Nate's eyelids flutter open so I can see his glittering amber eyes. He sees me and smiles.

"Morning," he mutters in a scratchy low voice.

"Morning? It's basically the afternoon," I say with a little laugh. Nate slowly moves into a seated position. I sit on the bed next to him.

"Really?" I show him the time on my phone and his eyes widen. "Oh shit." Nate looks at me. "You look comfy."

"Aw thanks," I say, hugging myself in his sweatshirt. "I plan on stealing this from you."

"Keep it," Nate says with a laugh. "Looks better on you anyway." He gets up and pulls on a pair of sweats. I stand up and meet him next to his closet, putting my hands on his chest. He looks down at me with a wide smile.

"Any chance we could do that again?" I ask him.

"Absolutely," Nate purrs, lightly kissing me. I put on my jeans from last night and gather my clothes, throwing them in a drawstring bag I find in the corner of his room. Nate puts on a RU shirt and helps me pack my things.

"Let's get some food," he suggests, handing the bag to me and opening the door of his dorm.

The entire walk down to the dining hall is silent as the two of us let last night sink in. I realize when we're in the elevator that I must look like a mess, but as long as I act like I'm supposed to look this way, I don't think I'll be given a second look. I'm also sure I won't be the only one looking like this.

When we enter Rodgers, we swipe our I.D.s and get a booth tucked away in the corner of the dining hall. I get a plate and fill it with fruit and a muffin. I also get a glass of water and sit back down to wait for Nate to get an omelet from the made-to-order bar.

"So, when are we going to look at the orphanage documents?" I ask Nate after he sits down.

"I can't today. It's Sunday. I have to go to the house," he says, rolling his eyes.

"You're really going to face Brendon after last night?"

"If he's as smart as he likes to think he is, he'll skip the meeting today," Nate says tartly, taking a bite of eggs.

"I hope he does," I echo, eating a piece of watermelon.

"Hey, when did you talk to him before last night?" Nate asks.

"The first party you brought me to, remember? You apparently give him a bad feeling," I say in a mocking creepy voice.

Nate scoffs. "What an ass. He's got secrets too, but you don't see me announcing them to people," Nate says, clearly annoyed.

"Like what?" I ask, leaning in.

Nate smiles to himself. "His last girlfriend? Yeah, she was sleeping with two other guys behind his back," Nate says with a smirk. "And then he got sad and cheated on her, and she found out because he didn't shut up about it." My jaw drops. "Like I told you, he's not as smart as he likes to think he is."

"Wow." It's quiet for a bit as we both eat our food.

"You can go through the documents without me. It's alright."

"Okay. You *sure* you're alright with that?"

"One hundred percent. I know you're excited to look at them, and I kind of took the opportunity away from you last night."

"But what we did was *so* much more fun than looking at documents," I reassure him.

Nate laughs and his eyes sparkle. "Oh totally." I bite my lip and smile at him. For a moment, I get sucked into his eyes. They're a perfect shade of amber in the sunlight coming in from the window of the dining hall. It's right then that I decide I could stare into his eyes for the rest of my life. Nate seems to share the same feeling as he gazes longingly at me.

"Why are you looking at me like that?" I ask him with a laugh. Nate looks at me sneakily and leans in.

"Perce–"

"Morning guys!" interrupts Finn, walking over to our table. "Mind if I sit?"

"Sure. Have a seat," I say, somewhat let down. Finn sits down next to me. Nate's leg starts to bounce nervously. The bouncing subtly shakes the whole table.

"So, I've met you in passing, but haven't actually *met* you," Finn says, looking at Nate and taking a bite of his bagel. "I'm Finn Larson. I'm an engineering major."

"I'm Nate Stevenson and a journalism major," introduces Nate.

"Aren't you the one in the frat?" Finn questions with a smirk.

"Finn," I snap softly.

"What? I just asked him a question," Finn says. As I look at him, I can see a little gleam in his eyes. He's up to something.

"Yeah I'm in Delta Rho," says Nate slowly.

"So are *you* the one who's trying to get Brook to solve the SHA murder?" Finn asks. I almost spit out my food, and Nate practically chokes on his omelet. My head snaps to Finn as he looks calmly at my boyfriend.

"Um, no. I actually didn't even know she was trying to solve anything," Nate smoothly lies. He looks across the table at me as though what Finn is telling him is brand new information. Finn takes another bite of his bagel.

"Yeah, she's risking her life to find out what happened to *your* people," Finn says accusingly. I look at Finn incredulously.

"*My* people? You alright, dude?" Nate laughs, looking at me like this interrogation is a joke.

"Finn, enough!" I exclaim.

"Look, I fully understand that Brook thinks you're a good person, but for some odd reason, you give me a *horrible* feeling, Stevenson," Finn says.

"That seems to be a recurring theme," Nate says tightly.

"Jesus, Finn," I snap.

Finn puts his hands up in surrender. "Brook, I'm just asking questions!"

"Well, alright, can you ask them in a way that doesn't make you sound like an asshole?" I say. Nate coughs in surprise as he's taking a drink of coffee.

Finn looks at me with a pointed expression. "Brooklyn, you know me. If I feel like something's off, I have to say something. And right now, this guy isn't sitting well with me," says Finn, glancing at Nate who's wiping coffee off of his mouth.

"You know, if you hate me so much, why are you here?" Nate asks, looking at Finn.

"Because Brooklyn's my friend," Finn says.

"Finn, you need to leave," I say.

"I'm not–"

"That *wasn't* a suggestion, Finn! Now go!" I yell. Finn gets up, throws Nate one last dirty look, then leaves us alone. I sit back in my seat and groan.

Nate looks at me. "Seems like a nice kid." Nate says it so nonchalantly that I start to laugh. Pretty soon, we're both laughing so hysterically that people around us start to wonder if we're okay.

※ ※ ※

"So, you finally slept with Nate?" Drew says, jumping to the end of her bed as I return to my dorm. I give her a sneaky look, and Drew nods her head approvingly. "Kenni owes me ten bucks."

"You had bets going?" I exclaim, putting Nate's bag full of my stuff down on my bed.

"Oh, yeah. Kenni's gonna be pissed. She guessed it was gonna be next week," Drew snickers. I roll my eyes and change out of Nate's sweatshirt, throwing it into my closet. "Were you drunk?"

"Oh no, we were both completely sober," I tell her.

"Damn, now *I* owe *her* five bucks," Drew grumbles.

I flop onto my bed and stare at the blank ceiling before breaking out into a huge smile. My hands cover my face as I start giggling. "He was so amazing," I say through my fingers.

"Alright I get it." Drew gets off of her bed and picks up Finn's papers on my desk. "Let's figure this out."

I roll over onto my stomach then push myself up into a seated position. "I'm happy I thought to print them out. Someone deleted the email."

Drew widens her eyes. "Damn. And there's no way you could've gotten those alone. So does the guy who's after you knows that Nate is helping?" Drew asks. I nod.

"And he might know that you're helping too. Have you told anyone?" I ask her.

Drew shakes her head. "God no. I can't die. I still have the high point of my career to reach," says Drew.

I roll my eyes and sit down at my desk. "Okay let's see what we've got here," I say with a sigh.

We start by looking at Finn's mother who went to Resslar. She apparently had Finn and gave him up when she was 19. She also was diagnosed with depression and had a possible schizoaffective disorder as well.

When Drew reads that, she winces. "God, can that be inherited?" Drew asks.

"Google it," I demand.

Drew goes over to her computer and looks it up. "It doesn't seem like that can be inherited per se, but the fact that your parent had it makes you more vulnerable for that sort of stuff. It also doesn't seem to make you violent either, which is good for her case," Drew reads off as she scrolls through her search.

"Alright," I say. I keep perusing the document in front of me. Finn's mom had a blood type of O negative and had bright blue eyes like her son. That little piece of information suddenly makes me aware of what I'm doing. Finn would actually *kill* me if he knew what I was up to. My accessing these records and poking into his family history would destroy him. In fact, the morality of most of what I've been doing thus far is questionable. *If my father could see me now…*

Drew's voice snaps me out of my train of thought. "Hey, so, I'm taking a look at his dad," she says in a questioning tone. "What was the day the frat brother died?"

I get out the stack of CP summaries and leaf through them until I find the right one. "March 27th, 1997 at 3 in the morning at Saint Joseph Hospital," I recite from the notes. "Why do you ask?"

"Because Scott Michale died on March 27th, 1997," Drew trembles, looking at the records. I look up at Drew in shock, my heart practically stopping. We're silent as we stare at each other in disbelief.

"There's no way," I whisper finally.

"Wanna bet?" Drew grabs Finn's mother's records off of the desk. "When did baby Finn get dropped off at Lakewood?"

"Does it say that in there?" I say, craning my neck to look at the papers. Drew flips through to the second page of documents, and I see her eyes skim the words on the page until she points at something.

"March 29th, 1997," she says almost inaudibly. The two of us just stare at the date.

"Is Finn's mom still around?" I breathe. Drew looks through and shakes her head.

"I can't tell. Seems like she hasn't given a health report since '97 because this is the most updated version they have. It's like she disappeared or something. Did you ask for the most recent one?" Drew says. I nod. I can't speak because my brain is on overdrive connecting the dots. I put my hands to my mouth in a praying position as I try to figure this out.

Finn was born on March 20th when his mom was 19. His dad was killed on March 27th, a week after Finn was born. Finn's mom gave him to the orphanage on March 29th and then got out of the picture. She may be in hiding because she's ashamed she was a teen mom or regrets giving Finn up. The mom also has a schizoaffective disorder that causes mood swings and abrupt changes in psychological behavior. Finn doesn't like talking about his biological parents because he hates them. He would never willingly seek them out. Finn was told his parents were in Greek life. That information wouldn't be on the forms we have. Unless—

I suddenly look up at Drew who has been staring at me in shock this entire time.

"We need to go to WRDW," I say definitively.

16

Drew and I run all the way to the station, our hair flying behind us. I can hear Drew take massive breaths as she runs, but I'm so focused on what lies in WRDW that I have to remind myself to breathe. When I swipe us into the station, I look to my left and to my right, checking if there are any familiar faces.

"Hey Brook!" calls Ryker, coming at me from my left suddenly enough that I jump. He looks surprised that I'm here on a Sunday afternoon, but also happy that I've decided to stop by. "What brings you here?" I see him suspiciously surveying my outfit of crappy jeans and a ratty RU t-shirt.

"Ryker, where's the room with the frat pictures in it?" I say hurriedly.

"Upstairs. Why—?" I lead the way up the stairs, Drew and Ryker following close behind. I go down the hall and through the doorway of the fraternity room where all of us stop and stare. Pictures of Greek life kids hang on the walls in neat rows, their eerie smiling 2-D faces staring at us. The pictures that didn't fit on the wall are in boxes on the floor, some stacked three high. I look around and nod affirmatively.

"We're looking for Scott Michale and Monica Earnest. Go," I order.

The three of us set to work tearing the room apart, Drew looking at the pictures on the wall as Ryker and I

163

rip through the boxes. Although I'm wary of having Ryker help, I figure he already knows what I'm up to because he sat in on half of the meeting I had with Peter. Drew is searching through the pictures on the walls and then stops.

"Wait, I think I have something!" she yelps. Ryker and I turn to her as she slumps her shoulders. "Never mind. Wrong Monica." We turn back to our work and keep going. I get through two boxes and Ryker gets through three before he rests his back against the wall.

"Why are we looking for these people?" he questions.

"The SHA case," I say simply. Ryker snorts. "What?"

"So, I'm part of your investigative team now?" he asks. Drew gives me an excited glance.

"I guess so," I relent.

Ryker smiles approvingly. "Dope. Let's keep going," he says. The three of us continue to look through the boxes. It would help if they were labeled but they aren't. Whoever set up this room just threw the pictures and names on their plaques into boxes and pushed the boxes against the wall. It might've seemed like a good idea at the time, but when someone needs to actually find something, it's infuriating to search.

"You said Scott Michale?" Drew reiterates, taking a picture out the pile of photos that Ryker already went through. I whip around to look at her.

"I thought I looked at that one," Ryker says with slight confusion. I rush over and kneel down beside Ryker as the three of us at the picture. Sure enough, there's a blonde male with Finn's winning smile kneeling in the third row of men. The little plaque at the bottom says 'SIGMA ETA ALPHA FRATERNITY-FALL PLEDGE CLASS 1996' before listing the names of the boys in the picture. I just stare at the picture in disbelief. Ryker gulps.

"Oh my God," Drew says with a breath out. "That's him."

"That's him," I agree. I take the picture gently from Ryker's hands and set it aside. "Let's look for his mom."

"If she's even here," Drew says, going back to looking on the walls.

"Do you guys know if Monica was in a sorority?" Ryker asks, closing the box of pictures we found Scott in and pulling out another one from the pile.

"We're working under the assumption that both of them were in Greek life. Let's exhaust all of our options before we search for her somewhere else," I instruct.

The three of us spend another fifteen minutes searching through boxes without any success. I can tell Drew is getting tired studying pictures of people who all are starting to look the same. I still don't know why Ryker is still here other than the possibility that he has nothing else to do. He has a look of intense concentration on his face and that amount of intensity is scaring me a bit, like when Nate was glaring down Brendon the other night.

"Brook!" Drew chokes out, looking into a box. Ryker and I look up at her from the floor. Drew nods at me, and I get up to look where she's looking. Sure enough, there's a woman with blonde hair and blue eyes in the back row of a group of about ten girls. The plaque reads 'KAPPA ALPHA DELTA SORORITY-FALL PLEDGE CLASS 1996.' Monica's name is engraved in little letters in the list of names below the picture.

"Here," says Ryker, handing me the picture of Finn's dad. When I put the two pictures side by side, I almost scream.

I can see Finn's hard jawline in Scott, Finn's softer cheeks in Monica, Finn's nose in his dad, and Finn's sparkling blue eyes in his mom. If the two of them had a child, it would be Finn for sure.

We found Finn's parents.

All of a sudden, everything makes sense.

"Holy shit," I whisper. I start to pace around the room, trying to avoid the boxes all over the floor. Ryker and Drew watch me walk around with their arms crossed over their chests. "Holy shit! I got it!"

"Yeah?" Drew says, confused.

"Yeah!" I confirm.

"Explain."

"Scott and Monica were dating before coming to RU. It says on those forms they were born in the same town. They came here together and they both rushed in the fall of 1996. Meanwhile, Monica is diagnosed with a schizoaffective disorder. And at the same time, all of the SHA hazing shit happens. Monica comes to college pregnant and doesn't tell Scott until she's showing because she's afraid that he won't want to keep it," I say, my brain thinking faster than my mouth can speak.

"This actually makes sense," Drew nods. Ryker looks lost as hell.

"So, Monica has the baby and Scott freaks out at her because she didn't tell him. Monica realizes Scott won't help care for the baby at all since he didn't want a kid in the first place. He somehow dies, she realizes she looks like a suspect because they were arguing, and she has emotional issues that people think could lead to violence. She leaves school and gives Finn up."

Drew and Ryker are silent as I look at them with wild eyes.

"You got all that from pictures?" Ryker finally says.

"No. We have the medical records of these two," I quickly waive off. Ryker raises his eyebrows. "I'll tell you more later if you want me to, but Drew that makes sense!"

"You know, it actually does. And I don't know how the hell you just figured that out. But still, why would someone be after you? The public knows a kid died in the house that was beating the crap out of the brothers already. Why are you suddenly Public Enemy Number One?" Drew asks.

"Wait, hold on. Someone's *after* you?" Ryker repeats incredulously. I lean against the wall with my arms crossed, my eyes searching the ceiling for an answer like I didn't even hear him.

"It's a whole thing," Drew says in a low voice to him.

"Does she usually do this?" Ryker whispers to Drew, not taking his eyes off of me.

"Yeah, but I don't know how she—" I cut Drew off.

"We were right!" I say with a little laugh. "Monica was framed. There's no way she could've killed him, she was carrying their kid. It was easy to blame her. She acted suspicious because of everything and because the father of her kid died. Someone else killed Scott and that's what my stalker is trying to keep me away from."

"Your *what*?" Ryker says perplexed.

"So, what? You think a bunch of 40-year old ex-frat guys are out to get you?" asks Drew, blowing past him.

"No, no. There must be something else to this." I keep pacing, biting my thumb nail as I think.

"Stop pacing, Brooklyn. You're scaring me," says Ryker.

I stop and look straight ahead. "That's it. I *scare* them," I say, looking over at them.

"So?" Drew asks. "What matters at this point is not *why* you're scaring them, but *who* you're scaring. And there's no way to tell that without..." I give her a mischievous look which she responds to by backing up and putting her arms by her side. "No. Brooklyn, I know what you're thinking and no."

"How else are we going to figure out who's after me?" I ask.

Drew looks at Ryker. "You're her boss! Can't you tell her this is a stupid idea?" she pleads.

Ryker looks between Drew and me. "I'm sorry, I don't have roommate telepathy. What's going on here?" Ryker says.

"Ryker!" Our three heads whip around to Lukas with Sydney at his side. They're looking down at the mess we've created on the floor. Sydney is staring down Drew like she somehow knows my roommate is an outsider. Drew notices because she gives Sydney a look daring her to do something about it.

"What the hell is happening here?" Syd challenges, breaking eye contact with Drew to look with confusion around the room.

"Sleuthing," I say simply, shrugging a bit.

Lukas pushes his glasses up his nose. "Alright. You gonna clean this up?" he asks.

"Yes *Mom*," says Ryker, rolling his eyes.

"Shut up," Lukas quickly retorts in a bored tone.

"We need you downstairs as soon as you clean this up," Syd requests. With that, Lukas and Sydney leave.

"They sound like fun," says Drew sarcastically, bending down to pick up plaques.

Ryker snorts. "Yeah he's a great guy." He looks at me. "Hey Brook, can I talk to you outside for a second?"

"Sure." The two of us leave Drew alone in the room and walk down the hallway a bit so we have some distance from the open door. As soon as we're far enough away, Ryker starts in with the questioning.

"What are you planning? Who's coming after you?" he interrogates.

"If I'm right about this Monica theory, someone is after me for getting all of that right," I answer.

"Like, someone wants to *hurt* you?" Ryker whispers with wide eyes. I nod. "Who?"

"I'm not sure yet, so keep this under the radar," I warn. I try to go back to the room, but he grabs my forearm and looks at me with scared eyes.

"I'm not done," he says. "Look, I know Peter said you could look into this, but this is serious if someone is after you."

"I know. I'm trying to figure this out before I'm next," I half-heartedly joke. I make a move to go again, but Ryker's grip tightens.

"Brooklyn," he cautions in a serious voice.

"Ryker," I say, mocking his tone. Ryker looks into my eyes, sighing through his nose. The concerned look on his face makes something in my stomach turn. *What's wrong with him?*

"I just... I just don't want to see you hurt," he relents in a simpering tone.

I nod slowly. "Alright," I say, drawing out the word as I survey his face.

Ryker seems to have noticed that he hasn't stopped staring at me. He clears his throat and shakes his head slightly, but his grip doesn't give. "If you need help with anything whether it be research, sorting through attics, or fending off some burly asshole, call me. I'll be there," he promises.

I give him a relieved smile. "I will," I say.

"And, you know, keep me in the loop with this stuff."

"Will do," I confirm, saying anything just to make him let go. Ryker's grip loosens enough at that point where I can slip through his fingers and go back to the room to find that Drew is tidying up a box of plaques. The wooden slabs stick out at odd angles like a teetering Jenga tower.

"Oh, thanks for the help." She stands up and cleans her hands on her jeans. "They really need to dust these every once in a while," she comments. Ryker arrives in the doorway by my side. He puts his hand on the small of my back, and it catches me by surprise. It scares me so much that I jump, causing him to pull his hand away. Drew raises her eyebrows. "All good?"

"Yeah." I turn around to Ryker, giving him a confused glance. The fact he's touched me more than he ever has makes me want to grab him and ask what's wrong, but a part of me already knows. My stomach churns even more when I see there's a bit of purpose to the way he looks down at me. "Ready to go, Drew?"

"Ready as ever." She says it while looking wistfully at Ryker who's rolling up his sleeves as he gets ready to clean up the rest of the floor. I clear my throat and she nods at me. "Yeah let's go."

"Thank you so much Ryker," I say.

My boss looks up from the floor. "Yeah no problem. And you both have my number so if either of you need anything, just let me know."

"Oh, we will," flirts Drew with a little smile. I roll my eyes and practically have to drag her away from him. "It's always go, go, go with you, isn't it? We can't take time to look at the pretty boy?" Drew groans in exasperation once we're making our way home on the sidewalk.

"He's my boss," I remind her. "And how can you think of a hot guy right now?"

"I don't know, Brooklyn. Maybe it's because the hot boy wants to help us!" Drew points out.

"I don't think he does, Drew," I say in a slow voice.

"Why not?"

"The first call I got from my stalker was right after Ryker dropped me off at home a few weeks ago," I say.

"Yeah so?"

"*So,* I asked him about the SHA house on the car ride over and then I got out of the car and no more than fifteen minutes later, I got a call from someone telling me to stop asking about it," I recount. "And now, he's being weird about me digging into this and tells me to keep him updated."

"If he's involved in trying to kill you, then why would he offer to help us and why would he continue to see you on a regular basis at the station?" Drew reasons. I consider what she says and Drew shakes her head. "First Finn and now Ryker? Brooklyn, I think you're looking in the wrong places."

17

On Monday morning, I meet Nate in front of our COM134 class so he can kiss me hello before we enter the room. There's the usual low chatter of my peers talking about their weekend and the usual guys in the back boasting about how much they drank before they blacked out. I take out my notebook and flip to where I last wrote, getting ready to take notes as the professor pulls up his slideshow on the screen.

"So, when are you going to tell me what you found?" Nate asks quietly, turning around in his seat to look at me.

"After class," I assure him.

Nate looks at someone coming down the aisle. "If you make it that far," he mutters before turning back around. I hear Taylor drop his bag unceremoniously onto the floor before he dramatically slams into the only open seat in the room with a big sigh. I keep my eyes on the slideshow the professor is presenting. Taylor, clearly pissed that I'm not giving him attention, groans as he takes out his laptop from his bag which weighs a lot less than he's making it seem. Finally, his brutish noises tip me over the edge.

"What?" I snap.

"And hello to you too, Brooklyn," says Taylor kindly. "Did you have a nice weekend?"

"You don't care," I say.

"You're right. I don't!" Taylor looks at me with a smug smile. "How did you get to be so smart, Brooklyn?"

"I listen and learn at a school that my parents pay a lot of money for me to attend. You should probably do the same," I say. I hear Nate snort from in front of me. Taylor gives me a dirty look and starts to pound out notes into his computer. I look over at his laptop and notice two little black lines on his skin sticking out of his rolled-up sleeve.

Taylor looks over at me. "What are you staring at?" he growls.

"Your arm," I say. "Did you get a tattoo over the weekend?" Taylor looks at his left forearm and moves the sleeve down so the little lines aren't sticking out anymore.

"Yeah, I did. Not telling you what it is though because *you don't care*," he jeers.

"You're right. I don't!" I say, mocking the tone he used earlier. We both groan at each other and look back at the slideshow about the history of advertising.

🐝 🐝 🐝

"Isn't it exhausting arguing with him all the time?" Nate asks me after class, handing me a cup of coffee as he does so.

"At the risk of sounding like a first grader, he started it, Nate!" I say in a voice that comes out whinier than I mean it to.

Nate snorts and takes a sip of his coffee from Newsworthy. "Alright, so what did you find?"

I tell Nate everything about the documents and how we ran to WRDW to search through the pictures of the old Greek life kids and then found Finn's parents in the pictures. I leave out the part about Ryker's hand on my back which, if I think about it for too long, I can feel on my skin. When I'm done, Nate whistles. "Seems like you found Finn's parents and they're at the center of this thing," he recaps. "Are you gonna tell him?"

"Yeah I'm going to tell the guy that didn't want me to do this that I found his parents and they're connected to one of the worst things in the history of this school," I say sarcastically.

"But Brook, you found his *biological parents*. And one of them is *dead*. Shouldn't he know that much?" Nate asks.

"Do *you* want to explain to him how we figured out that it was his parents? Me neither," I agree in response to his head shaking a bit.

Nate sighs and takes a sip of coffee. "Alright, so what's next?"

"I'm so glad you asked," I say in a happy tone. Nate looks confused. "So, I figure we've got most of the story, but there has to be something else that we're missing. I don't think Monica killed him like the cops said. I also still don't know who's after me. And the only way we can know what we're missing and call the cops on whoever's after me is if we go into the house." Nate quickly swallows the gulp of coffee he just took and looks at me with an open mouth.

"Brooklyn," he says after a pause. "You can't—"

"I know how crazy that sounds, but I've gone to every other place on campus besides inside the actual house," I push.

"There are a *million* reasons why this is *horrible* idea, the least of which being there's a Campus Police

Officer who hates you and wants an excuse to write you up," Nate hisses.

"Greenwood won't know we're there," I reassure him. Now Nate looks even more worried.

"*We*?!"

"Yes 'we'! You, me, and Drew." Nate puts his head in his hands and rubs his temples. "Or I'll just go by myself."

"No!" Nate jumps. "The last thing I want you to do is go into that house by yourself." He puts his head back in his hands. "But the last thing *I* want to do is get expelled and kicked out of DR."

"We're going to go at, like, one in the morning. Maybe two if we're late. I promise no one will see us." Nate chews on the inside of his cheeks as he thinks it over.

"How are we going to get in?"

"Some windows on the first floor are boarded up, no nails or screws or anything. The boards are jammed in the frame. We'll just take out the plywood and replace it when we go in."

"And if we get caught?" Nate asks.

"Run like hell," I say. Nate laughs and keeps his head in his hands. It's quiet as he's letting my proposition set in.

"Run like hell," he repeats. "Great advice."

"Thanks," I say proudly. Nate looks into my eyes hopelessly. I reach across the table and take by boyfriend by the hand. "Please Nate."

Nate shakes his head. "Do we seriously have to do this? Don't you have some suspects already?"

"Not really. I think Greenwood is somehow involved in it. And then of course Finn, but Drew says he would never do anything like this. Drew also likes Finn though,

so of course she would say he's innocent. And then..."
I trail off, thinking of Ryker.

"And then?" Nate prompts.

"My boss at the radio station could be involved. But there's no connection that I can figure out between him and the house. I don't know why he would want to defend it to the point of threatening me with murder," I reason aloud.

Nate shakes his head as he finishes off his coffee. "Your boss? That guy loves you. And you said he's even *helping* you. There's no way. I would look into your buddy more than your boss." I bite the inside of my cheek as I think of his thought process.

"Alright. Let's go back home. I want to look over my notes again."

The two of us walk across campus back to our building. While Nate talks about the dynamic between Brendon and another frat brother, I keep thinking about Drew's defense of Finn. It would make the most sense if he wants to kill me considering he's made it *perfectly* clear that he'd rather me keep my nose out of the situation. Although, Finn's major would make it difficult for him to keep constant tabs on me.

Nate and I approach the front of Smith, and I'm about to kiss Nate goodbye when I spy the C.P. car in front of our building.

"You've got to be kidding me," I say slowly as I see Greenwood come out of the car. When he slams the door shut and faces the building, his eyes fixate on me and Nate who's standing sideways with his hand on my waist as he's looking at the officer.

"Is that Greenwood?" Nate says, his nose twitching. The officer rests his forearms on the top of his car and looks at me.

"Yep," I whisper to Nate. Greenwood comes up onto the sidewalk.

"Hey there, Perce," says the cop. "This your building?" Greenwood asks, nodding to Smith.

"Yes Sir," I say, remembering to add 'Sir' so he doesn't make me say it. "What brings you up here?"

"Just doing the routine rounds. The guy who's normally on the route is sick," says Greenwood. He lays eyes on Nate who's still looking at the officer like he's the plague. "And who's this fine gentleman?"

"Nate Stevenson," introduces Nate, keeping a wary eye on the officer as he goes to shake his hand.

"Boyfriend?" Greenwood asks.

"Yeah," Nate confirms, putting his hand back in his pocket.

"You got your hands full with this one." Greenwood looks down at me. "She doesn't know when to stop." He kicks a rock out of the way. "So, Mia told me the actual documents you took out the other day. Why are you so interested in the SHA murder?"

"I'm doing a story for WRDW. A twenty years later kind of thing," I say.

"Ah." Greenwood smirks. "You trying to solve it?"

"No," I lie. "Just interested."

"So why did this one look scared when I said that?" Greenwood says, nodding to Nate and snapping his gum with a smile. I don't break, but Greenwood's smile grows like he's caught me in a lie. "You really like lying to me, huh?"

"Not at all. I just don't know who might have a motive," I say, looking at the officer with a small smirk as I search his face.

Greenwood's smirk breaks into the toothy smile of a wolf. "You don't need a motive. Sometimes just a strong hatred of a person is enough to do it." He looks perfectly intimidating. On the outside, my face doesn't break, but on the inside, I'm screaming. Nate notices me tense up and he puts a reassuring hand on my back. Greenwood shrugs. "That's what I've seen on the force anyway."

"Of course," I say slowly. "We have to go. Until next time, Officer." I turn towards my building and walk with determination up the stairs. Once I get into the lobby, I peek out of the window to see if he's still there. Sure enough, Greenwood is on the phone talking to someone and looking up at my building. I swallow hard, praying the phone in my pocket doesn't go off. Thankfully, it doesn't. However, I see the officer look up at my dorm room window, then look through the window straight into my eyes.

It's enough to make me sick.

18

I get up the next morning and take a deep breath, savoring the fresh air.

"You know, we don't have to do this," Drew reminds me nervously at breakfast after not speaking to me for the entire morning. I look at my plate and say nothing, poking at my eggs which are runny from the water they were cooked in. "Brooklyn, I know you feel obligated to figure this out for Finn's dad's sake or whatever, but I'm telling you we do *not* have to break into that house." I flick my eyes up to meet hers. Her lips are tightly pursed, an expression I've never seen on my roommate.

"Drew, we need to do this. And I'll go alone if I need to," I reiterate. Drew heaves a big breath outward and puts her hands behind her neck.

"No, you can't go alone," she admits in a defeated tone.

"Nate's coming too," I tell her. Drew looks at me and scoffs, showing me the smile that's been absent from her face this entire morning.

"The boyfriend is coming? Well now I have to go," she says. The two of us finally smile at each other before continuing to eat our breakfasts.

The entire day goes by in a blur. I sit through my food studies class and say nothing then I get up, walk to another building, then sit through my math class, and say nothing. I mindlessly do homework for my COM classes when I get back to my dorm and then I just sit and listen to music as I wait for the clock on the microwave to hit one in the morning.

Drew comes home somewhere in there and watches Netflix. She cuddles up in her blanket and only smiles grimly at me when I look over at her. Nate comes over around midnight. He's dressed in a black army-style jacket, black jeans, and black Timberlands. When he pokes his head into the room, I look up from staring at the floor and greet him with a smile. He beckons for me to join him in the hallway. I quietly get up and go to the door without Drew noticing.

"Hey," Nate says when the door shuts.

"Hey," I respond with a sigh.

"We're still doing this?" he asks reluctantly. I cross my arms and nod. He can tell I'm scared out of my mind. He puts his hand on my arm. "We don't have to, Brook. We *really* don't have to if you're scared."

"You know, I've heard that a lot today," I grimace. I look into my boyfriend's loving eyes. "I need to do this." Nate cracks a smile and shakes his head.

We go back inside the dorm room to find Drew pulling on her ripped black jeans and black leather jacket. As Nate and I sit on my bed, she ties the laces on her black Converse and looks at two black baseball caps that are sitting on her desk. She seems like she's considering her options even though they look identical. Finally, she settles on the hat on the left, fitting it over her fading blue hair. She shuts her closet after perfecting her dark lipstick in the full-body mirror on the inside of the closet door. "What are you wearing, Brook?" I go to my closet and take off the RU shirt I was wearing to pull on a tight black tank top. I put a soft black hoodie over it. On the bottom, I opt for the darkest pair of jeans I own and put on my black knee-high combat boots. I see Nate glancing at me out of the corner of my eye.

"What?" I ask him. Nate shakes his head.

"Nothing," he says with a casual shrug. Drew makes a sound of disgust and hits him on the arm. I roll my eyes and shut my closet door then walk over to the two of them.

"Alright Brook. What's the plan?" Drew asks me, folding her arms across her chest.

"We get into the house, we try to find anything we can about the murder and about who might be stalking me, and we get the hell out," I sum up.

Nate nods. "Good plan. What if we get caught?"

"It's like I said. We get caught, run like hell and do *not* slow down or look back," I repeat. The three of us watch the clock on the microwave hit one A.M. I swallow hard when I see the numbers on the little screen.

"It's one in the morning on a Wednesday, and we're going to break into a house," Nate says like he's trying to convince himself this is actually happening. He goes to the fridge and takes out the bottle of Fireball that Drew has. Nate screws open the cap, puts the bottle to his lips, and takes a huge swig of the amber-colored liquid inside. He makes a face after he swallows the cinnamon-flavored liquor and puts the bottle back into the fridge. "Alright, I'm ready. Let's go."

"Boys," Drew scoffs as Nate confidently leads the way out of the door. I lock our dorm room and linger there for a second to remind myself to breathe.

We walk past the C.P. officer guarding the front door of our building without so much as a glance from him and meet the chilly night air as it hits our faces. Nate takes my hand and squeezes it as we walk under the streetlights down the driveway to our building. I can tell he's terrified by the way he's not letting go of my hand. If anything, he squeezes it tighter. Every step towards the house feels like a step backwards and every breath I take I cherish.

The three of us walk down the back stairs, past the tennis courts on our right, and arrive at the sidewalk across the street from the SHA house. We stare it down as it towers over us in all of its creepy glory. I grip Nate's hand harder and share an affirmative look with Drew who's standing on my right.

"Let's go," I declare in midst of a surge of courage. I cross the road and thank God that the students at Resslar don't party on Wednesday nights. There's no one outside except for us and the occasional bird, but even they freak me out as they quickly flit through the sky. I go around to the back of the house and look at a shattered window which is covered with a sheet of plywood. I look to Nate who proceeds to pry the piece of wood out of the window frame with his fingertips. It takes a bit, but he gets it open. When he finally takes it off, the smell of mold and stale air hits me. The inside of the frat house looks like a gaping pitch-black chasm that seems like it will swallow us whole upon entry.

Nate looks at it and then looks at me. "Ladies first," he whispers, jerking his head towards the window. I grip the sides of the window frame and pull myself up into the windowsill. My legs swing over and land on the wooden floor of the house with a cloud of dust erupting as the soles of my shoes hit it. I turn on my phone's flashlight as Drew comes into the house after me. Nate leaves the piece of plywood on the ground as he climbs into the window and once he's inside, he leans out of the window, grabs the wood, and wedges it back into place from the inside. When he does that, we're drowning in the darkness and silence, saved only by the pinpricks of our flashlights and our heavy breathing.

"Well this is creepy," mumbles Drew. We seem to have landed in a living room of sorts. Chunks of the ceiling are on the floor, exposing places that pipes would have been had they not been ripped out. The floor is dusty and cracking under our feet. I accidentally step on a floorboard and it creaks so loudly that I think my mom back home could hear. There's no furniture at all, though I can sort of see the outline on the floor made by the sun's rays beating on carpets. Spiders have made webs in every corner of the room. I wander into another space towards the front of the house that used to be a kitchen. The tile floor is busted, the countertops have caved in on themselves, and the wallpaper is peeling off. There are stains on the floor of where appliances used to be.

"Ugh!" Nate trembles as he opens the door to the bathroom. I walk over to him and look over his shoulder to see that a family of rats has nested in the empty toilet. He shuts the door and wipes the hand he used to open it on his jacket.

"What are we looking for?" Drew hisses from the dining room.

"Anything that seems like it would be recent," I answer, looking in a closet, finding nothing, then shutting it.

"Hey, over here" Nate says softly. Drew and I come join him at the bottom of a flight of stairs in the corner of the kitchen. After a glance towards them, I lead the way up the rickety stairs, dodging holes the entire way up. Drew's foot almost falls through one but she's caught by Nate who's behind the two of us.

We come into a hallway the runs perpendicular to the stairwell. The hallway seems to be full of bedrooms that the boys once occupied. I go to the right as Drew and Nate go to the left. I poke my head into each room and find that they're eerily empty. Some have beer cans in the corner or graffiti on the walls, but nothing seems suspicious. I glance into a very empty hall closet and find nothing out of the ordinary. When I shut it, I hear an unmistakable *THUD* behind the door. Quickly, my hand opens the door again, but there's still nothing there.

"What?" Nate asks, coming over to me and shining a light into the space. I enter the closet and softly knock on the sides until I hear a space that sounds hollow. Drew joins Nate at the door and the two of them watch me pry the back of the closet off with my fingertips.

"Holy hell," Drew breathes when I take off the entire panel that has been covering up three paddles, all of them decorated with Greek letters. There's some sort of dried red substance staining the ancient wood. A set of chills shoots up my spine and makes me step back. I set the wood aside, close the closet, and try to shut my mouth, but I can't.

Nate swallows hard. "Let's keep going," he says. I nod and keep walking down the hallway with the two of them behind me. Every door on either side of the hallway is open. We inspect the room behind each one, but there's nothing like the scene in the closet. Just when I'm about to venture back to the stairs, I notice the door to the room at the very end of the hallway is closed.

Drew shakes her head. "You are *not* going in there," she warns. Nate approaches to the door first and puts his ear up to it. He shakes his head and then stands back, motioning for Drew and me to do the same. In one swift motion, Nate kicks open the door and bursts into the room. Drew and I share a look of fear as we follow him inside.

In the middle of the floor is a crate that looks like it has been used as a table. Unlike the rest of the house, the floor in this room isn't dusty at all and the window is slightly open. Someone's been in here. The closet doors are absent, so we can see the floor inside has been taken out. When I shine my flashlight down the hole, a wooden ladder leading to the basement attached to the wall catches my eye. Drew gulps and quickly gets away from the hole. I feel it too; there's a chill coming up from the pit.

I return to the crate in the middle of the floor and open up the top. Inside are a handful of newspaper clippings, interview transcriptions, notes, and pictures. Not having time to sort through all of these, I take most of them and stuff the papers into my pockets.

"Holy shit, Brooklyn," Nate gulps, looking at the wall the door is on. I turn around with Drew and my heart almost stops. The little bit of moonlight coming in from the window illuminates the wall in question.

The wall that's covered in pictures of me.

I slowly walk towards the wall as my eyes search it. There I am outside of Rosenburg, outside of Smith, walking across the Quad, walking towards Cypress, sitting in Newsworthy. It doesn't seem like there was a moment when the stalker didn't get a picture of me. My stomach turns just thinking about the places he's seen me. My hand reaches up and takes a picture of me sitting on a bench outside of Rosenburg off of the wall. It's as if I've entered an inescapable waking nightmare. My hand feels detached from my body as I look at the picture of me.

"Nate, look," Drew breathes, pointing her flashlight towards the top right of the wall. Nate becomes angry when he sees the photos of him leaving the DR house, him sitting in front of the arts and sciences building, and him kissing me.

"They've got me too," Nate says in a hard voice.

"They've got all of us," I confirm, swallowing hard when I see a few pictures of Drew on the wall underneath Nate's section. There's even one of me talking to her and Kenni at lunch.

"There's no way one person could've taken all of these," I whisper.

"That means there's a group of 'em," Nate replies.

"And at least one of them is a student," Drew adds, pointing her flashlight at a picture of her entering the pottery studio in the basement of the art building. "You can't get into the studio unless you have an I.D." Her expression changes as she has a horrifying realization. "What if they're in my class?" The three of us just keep staring at the wall as though hypnotized. None of us can bring ourselves to turn away. I feel like my feet are super glued to the floor. I have to remind myself to breathe as I begin to hear a faint ringing in my ears.

"How many of them are there you think?" Drew asks.

"At least ten," Nate guesses. "This must be their hideout." I shake my head and hold it in my hands. As my fingers knot in my hair, I start to feel lightheaded. My throat closes as though I'm being suffocated. The air around me is having trouble reaching my lungs. This is too overwhelming. I don't even realize I've dropped to my knees until Nate crouches down beside me.

"Brook! Are you okay?" he whispers urgently. I put my hands on the floor and close my eyes, trying to establish a regular breathing pattern that my body can't quite seem to get a hold of. The ringing grows louder and louder. My hands jump to my ears and I squeeze my eyes tightly.

"We need to get out of here," Drew pushes, looking around.

Creeeeeak.

The three of our heads snap to look at the door. The ringing abruptly stops. My brain suddenly doesn't hurt anymore.

CREEEEEEAK.

I get to my feet and run to the ladder in the closet. Drew and Nate quickly follow suit and we clamber down the poorly constructed ladder that seems to be embedded in the wall. We pass what I assume is the wood surface of the first floor and then enter the basement. It smells musty and the air is so stale I actually have to stop myself from coughing. It's dark and wet and full of junk that probably has mold growing on it. I spy an old metal coat of arms in the corner that catches the awful lighting. It has two swords crossing at the bottom of it and the helmet of a knight on top that gives me the creeps.

Thump. Thump. Thump. Thump.

"Someone's here!" Drew mouths. I nod and look around the basement for a place to hide. Nate finally pulls Drew and me by the backs of our jackets into a closet and softly closes the door, leaving a crack open so we can see out. I clamp a hand around Drew's mouth since she's shaking like a chihuahua. Nate's hand finds mine in the darkness and we squeeze so hard I feel my circulation momentarily cut off. None of us move.

"She's getting closer," says a man's voice. I don't recognize it, mostly because I have to strain to hear it. Another person snorts.

"Nosey little bitch," says the snorter. I don't recognize that voice either, but the look on Nate's face indicates he might. I hear the two guys go up the stairs to the room we were just in. Their voices come in clearer since the line from the closet to the basement is wide open.

"She's been on us for too long. Why don't we just get her already?" laments the first guy, sounding disappointed.

"You know why," says the second. Nate looks at me and shakes his head. He knows I want to scream. The first guy chuckles.

"Eh, I guess he's right. She's kinda hot. I wouldn't mind seeing what I could to do her once we get her," he cruelly jokes. I open my mouth to yell, but Nate puts his free hand over my lips.

"I'll take her after you break her in," says the second guy with a deep chuckle. Nate makes the softest sound of discontent I've ever heard. "Alright, what are we looking for?"

"Notes or something. They must be around here somewhere," says the first.

"Who leaves that kind of shit just lying around? He's an idiot," says the other disdainfully.

"You wanna tell him that?" asks the first guy. There's the sound of moving papers. My stomach hurts and I can hear my blood pound in my ears. "Are these all of them?" There's more paper crinkling. "Thought there were more." Then the shuffling stops.

"Dude," says the second guy.

"What?"

"Look." There's silence. "There's one missing." My heart drops as the crumpled picture that I took from the wall suddenly weighs about a hundred pounds in my pocket. More silence.

"No there's not," says the first guy.

"Then how come there's a friggin' hole in the middle of the wall?" snaps the second. Silence.

"You don't think...?" the first one says slowly. The entire house stands still. The two guys stand there before walking determined in opposite directions. "You take upstairs, I'll go down. The little bitch better run."

"Oh my God," Nate breathes.

"YOU HEAR THAT, BITCH?" roars the first guy. "RUN FOR YOUR LIFE!"

Nate lets me go and the two of us burst out of the closet.

"Where do we go?" he hisses.

"Wait! Where's Drew?" I ask hurriedly.

THUD. THUD. THUD.

"Guys!" Drew yells as the footsteps come down the stairs. She's back inside of the closet, beckoning us in. We come over to her and see the huge hole in the side of the closet. It looks like a tunnel big enough for a human to walk through. We all look at each other, realize

189

it's our only option, turn on our flashlights, and take off into the darkness.

The three of us sprint through the tunnel that was clearly dug with shovels. Roots are exposed, side of pipes are protruding, worms and bugs are crawling everywhere, and the ground is muddy. As we go further and further into the tunnel, I wonder how long it took for the boys to dig this. It's *long*, but it's surprisingly wider than I would have expected. We must've been running for two or three minutes, but the tunnel keeps on going and going and going. Then it starts to go uphill.

"Jesus, how long is this thing?" Nate says from the front.

"Keep running!" Drew calls from behind me. We run uphill for about three minutes before I see a dim light ahead. The light gets closer and closer until—

"Shit!" exclaims Nate as he bursts into the light, takes out a few rocks with his side, and trips over a shovel. He groans in pain. I have to run to the side of him to avoid pushing him over. My roommate accidentally pushes my back when she emerges, sending the both of us to the ground. I yelp when I hit the tile floor and roll onto my back so my eyes can absorb the fluorescent lighting. Nate gives me a hand to help me up.

It seems like we've landed in a supply closet. Gloves and shovels are all over the floor. There are electrical boxes on the walls and pipes running over the ceiling. Drew looks around as she dusts herself off, clearly confused.

"Where the hell are we?" she asks. I carefully push the door to the closet open and see a long hallway.

The three of us file out and shut the door behind us. The thing has a keypad lock so when it slams shut, the electronic mechanism clicks. I try to make some sense of where we are, but I still fall short.

"Wait a minute," says Nate slowly.

He jogs down the hallway, and Drew groans. "Dude, I just ran uphill. Slow down," she complains. Nevertheless, the three of us reach the end of the hallway and look at a set of elevators.

"I don't believe it," Nate whispers. "This is the basement in Cypress. I thought the laundry was down here when I first moved in, but it's just for custodians. I got lost down here."

"This is how they get in and out of the house," I deduce, a small lightbulb going off inside of my head.

"Then how did those two get in?" Drew asks. There's silence that I break by putting my palm to my face.

"The window!" I say.

"What?" Nate asks.

"Like how we got in! You just pop the piece of plywood out of the frame and put it back in when you're done," I say.

"There's no way they all go in through a window when they have meetings," Nate reasons. "They must have the PIN to the door down here and go in through the tunnel."

"It's not scaring you that they have meetings in that house?" Drew says to me.

"Well, of course they have meetings! They need to be on the same page about stalking me!" I say, my voice becoming higher and higher the more excited I get.

"You know, this is the most thrilled I've seen someone when they figure out they're being stalked,"

Nate says as he pushes the button to call the elevator. I turn to him, my mind processing at a million miles an hour.

"You looked like you recognized one of their voices," I jump, turning to my boyfriend. "Who do you think it was?"

Nate shrugs. "I mean, I've met a lot of guys from rush. At some point, they all start to sound the same," he hesitates. He can see I'm let down. "If I knew the guy's name for certain, I would absolutely tell you," he reassures me, "but I don't want you guys chasing conspiracies. It's bad enough you think Finn and your radio station boss are in on it." The elevator door slides open and, thankfully, no one is inside.

"Not Ryker anymore," I say. "Greenwood."

"That freaking *cop*?" Drew exclaims.

"He literally said hatred is a good enough motive to hurt someone. He stared right at me when he said it. Nate saw!" I defend.

Nate nods begrudgingly. "It was spooky," he agrees. The elevator delivers us to Nate's floor. The three of us walk down the hallway and collapse once we get inside his room. We're covered in dust and dirt. Drew's eyes are red like she cried at some point. I sit on Nate's bed and take the picture of me out of my pocket. Nate sits next to me and puts his arm around my shoulder.

"We didn't figure out who's after me," I say softly.

"No, we didn't," Nate echoes.

"But we did figure out that if they're the ones after you, you can outrun them and that's all that matters," Drew says, still slightly huffing and puffing.

"Wait!" I blurt, remembering the papers in my pocket. I drop to my knees and uncrumple them, my friends helping me. "Alright, what do we have?" I scan the papers and quickly read over them. One is a newspaper article about Scott's death with the headline *SHA Brother Beaten to Death*. Drew swallows as she reads it. Another paper is an interview conducted by C.P. with Monica before she disappeared. The other papers I grabbed are just logs of times, places and dates which I assume are their meeting times. They look randomized. Nate shakes his head as he reads through the interview.

"Okay, so what is this? Monica said Scott hated the hazing process in the following spring. Why would he continue to be in the frat then?" Nate asks. He keeps reading. "They underlined the C.P. officer saying, 'How long have you known about your mental health issues?' and then Monica's answer is just crying. What a shitty question."

"You were wondering who framed Monica, Brook. Seems like it was C.P.," Drew says grimly.

I shake my head. "But they didn't think that through. Schizoaffective disorders don't cause you to be vio—" I stop abruptly as I remember the bloody SHA paddles in the closet. All of a sudden, something clicks. Nate and Drew look over at me, expecting me to finish my sentence.

"Scott Michale *did* die in a hazing ritual, because they *all* killed him. That's why they couldn't identify one person. The brothers collectively killed Scott," I breathe.

"You're kidding," Drew says in disbelief. I shake my head excitedly, turning to them.

"No. Monica was right. Scott hated the hazing process. Scott didn't go along with the hazing of new recruits in the semester following his initiation, so the brothers beat him in the head with those paddles and strangled him when he wasn't dying fast enough as an example. The brothers knew Monica on a more personal level like the Delta Rho guys know me. Scott must've told them about Monica's mental health and the pregnancy, so the members could feasibly say she went nuts and killed him." There's another pause so I can think, but also so I can breathe. "That's why the brothers are after me. They've been hiding behind their own lie since the nineties and the school was fine with letting that happen because the C.P. officers clearly didn't give a shit and were too incompetent to do anything. The administration didn't go after them because of financial reasons."

"If they lost the former brothers, they would lose donors," Nate chimes in.

"Exactly! Then when the cops tried to solve it, the brothers decided to not rat each other out. Why would you turn your *brother* in? Then cops and journalists dropped it 'cause they weren't getting anywhere and were too scared *they* would go missing when they heard about the one dead reporter. I'm just the first person to be nosy and persistent enough to figure this out."

"So, the people who keep calling you are who, exactly?" Nate asks.

"It's like Drew said before, they're students. They couldn't have gotten into any of the art building's labs without an I.D."

"Why would current students be in a defunct fraternity?" wonders Drew. It's quiet as I shake my head.

"I don't know," I whisper, swallow hard as I realize the consequence of my realization. "I guess that's the next thing to figure out." Nate's room is silent as all of us let the night sink in.

Ding ding. Ding ding.

My phone goes off in my pocket and my hand immediately grabs it. It's the unknown number. Nate and Drew seem terrified, but I steel my face and pick it up.

"Gotcha," I snarl.

"I said to stay away," says the voice, devoid of any emotion.

"Yeah, little late for that," I growl.

He's quiet, the silence hanging in the air like a fog. "Goodbye Brooklyn." He hangs up, and I put my phone on the ground, staring at it like it might explode.

19

"OH MY GOD, BROOKLYN!" Drew screams, bursting into our room Thursday afternoon and promptly collapsing on the ground. I automatically leap up from my desk and look at her, startled by her yelling.

"What happened? Is anyone hurt? Are you okay?" I shout.

"I am *more* than okay, my friend!" Drew gets up and bounces in place. It's like she drank Kenni amounts of caffeine. "Dex just asked me if I want to go grab coffee tonight like an actual date, and so now I have a date and he's going to pick me up in, like, twenty minutes and he lives in Cypress, so I have to move!" Drew goes to her closet and starts to tear through her clothes like a madman.

"That's amazing! How did he ask you?" I ask, thankful that it's not what I thought it was.

"I was texting him, and he just asked! I'm so excited. Can you believe it?" she squeals.

"I'm so proud of you!" I say in a genuine tone, getting back onto my bed.

"What do I wear?" Drew brings out two shirts from her closet and looks down at them. They look like the exact same V-neck tee to me. "Black or black?" I pretend to consider her options.

196

"The black on the right is darker, but the black on the left matches your eyes," I say. "I don't know, it's your call." Drew groans.

"Fine, the one on the right then." She throws on the shirt carelessly as I keep typing my essay for COM134. Drew puts her leather jacket over shirt, looks at me, and spins. "Do I look good?"

"Like the badass you are," I answer. Drew gives me a thumbs up.

When Dex comes by to pick up Drew, I'm taken aback by his looks, totally expecting someone else. Dex's long Bieber-Circa-2008 brown hair is in his eyes. He's taller and doesn't look like he has a lot of muscle on him. There are bags under his eyes like he hasn't slept in days. He's wearing a torn jean jacket with a loose white t-shirt underneath that hangs off of him like a sheet. His ripped black jeans stick to his legs, and his black boots are worn down to the point where they are fraying.

Drew gives him a winning smile when she opens the door. "Hello," she says sweetly.

"Hey," drawls Dex as though I'm hearing him in slow motion.

"Come in. Let me just touch up my make-up, and we'll go," Drew says. After he shuffles into the room, Dex looks around and awkwardly stands near the door, but judging by his appearance, I figure wherever Dex stands, he stands awkwardly. His tired eyes survey the space, and they finally rest on me. I feel his grimy stare from across the room, so I look over.

"Hey. I'm Dex," he says, waving lazily.

"I'm Brooklyn," I greet, giving him a tight smile. Drew finishes putting on makeup in her mirror and shuts the closet door in a final way.

"Okay let's go!" Drew says. Dex holds open the door for her and she waves good-bye to me from the hallway. The door shuts, and I'm left alone. I put on my headphones and turn up the music so my stalker can't haunt my thoughts.

I try to take a nap, but my dreams are plagued by a man with an axe who chases me through campus. No one around me seems to notice I'm being hunted, but the man keeps coming after me. I run myself ragged trying to escape him and his screams of fury, but he eventually corners me and brings the axe down on my head.

Drew comes back from her date two hours later and cannot shut up. She goes on and on about how the two of them have plans to go into Northwich and go to a serious restaurant together, not just a coffee house. She says something about wanting to do a project for class with him and wanting to go on a second date. She's completely smitten with Dex. I wish I could pay more attention to her, but I seem to have gone into survival mode. I can't think of anything else except how to escape a potentially dangerous situation with all of my limbs intact.

❄ ❄ ❄

On Friday, Drew throws a bag of junk food onto the floor of our dorm. I look up from the homework I'm doing and see her hang her leather jacket on a hook in a huff.

"I hiked those three bags of chips from the corner store that's about a mile across campus!" she grumbles, grabbing the plastic bag from the ground and throwing the chip bags into the shelf in her closet where we keep food. "They better be the best chips I've ever tasted!"

"Be a little more aggressive. I don't think you broke all of 'em," I tell her. Drew groans and flops onto her bed.

"Oh, shut it." She looks over at me. "How are you doing?"

"I'm fine. Just doing some math homework." I nod to the bags on the floor. "What's with the chips?"

"Dex and Kenni are coming over tonight for some scary movies. I needed to go to the corner store anyway, and I figured I would offer them some food. That's what a good hostess does, right?"

"Sounds like it."

Drew grabs her computer off of her desk. "I should do some homework too before he comes. Will I actually do it through? Probably not." A small *ding* sound comes from her computer and her face goes from bored to excited. "Oh my God, Ryker texted me!"

"What?" I say, thoroughly confused.

Drew reads the second text that just came in and her face falls. "Damn, it wasn't asking me to be his wife. He wants to know if you can come to work tonight," Drew reads, clearly disappointed. "Why is he asking me?"

"My phone is dead," I say, pointing to my charging phone on my desk. Her computer dings again, and she smiles happily.

"Dex says he's going to bring beer tonight," she informs me.

"Sounds good. Do you mind if I go to WRDW later? I shouldn't be more than an hour or two. You guys can start without me." Drew groans.

"Alright. If you *must* go hang out with my future husband, I guess I can't stop you." She types Ryker an answer back and then looks at his reply. "He says to come at eight."

"Okay," I confirm. Drew puts down her laptop, walks over to the fridge, and pulls out the bottle of Fireball we have. She fills up a shot and throws it back. When I raise an eyebrow, Drew shrugs.

"Might as well loosen up before tonight," she says.

A few hours later, I put on a black jacket over my grey tank top. I don't change out of my ripped jeans since I'm assuming I won't see anyone important at the station. I put on tall brown boots and stuff my I.D. and wallet into the pocket of my jacket.

"Bye Drew," I say, waving good-bye to my roommate.

"Bye! See you later!" she says.

I walk through the lobby, bracing myself for the cold which hits like a slap to the face once I walk outside. I flip my hood up to protect my cheeks against the biting wind and keep my head down so my hood isn't blown back. I walk past the SHA house and stare it down like I usually do. Lately, I've been immersing myself in homework and essays. I'm almost too scared to go back to the case. I haven't seen Greenwood in a while, so I'm assuming the cop has stopped trying to bust me for the time being. He's probably on patrol considering it's Friday night. Although the parties don't start until at least eleven, some houses that I walk past are blasting music and are holding screaming people who are ready to go out in a couple hours. When I look down the street, I see the DR house is getting ready to host later. I feel bad for abandoning Drew and Kenni with the creepy

Dexter, but Drew seems to be comfortable with him and I can't say no to work, especially if I want to be head of the station someday. After fumbling for my I.D., I manage to swipe in and hurry inside.

The WRDW station is empty, except for an unknown student in charge of the boards in the production room who is controlling the programming. I wander into the newsroom and see Ryker on his laptop. His feet are up on the desk, and his back is towards me. I can see the screen he's looking at is split between a text conversation and a Microsoft Word document with what I'm guessing is a story on it. I knock on the door frame three times and Ryker turns around.

"There she is!" he says in a somewhat startled tone, shutting his laptop and crossing his arms. "Thank you so much for coming in. No one else wanted to."

"I wasn't doing anything tonight anyway," I say. I nod to the computer. "Who are you texting?"

"Oh, that?" Ryker looks back at his computer. "That's just Peter. He wants to know how everything's going."

"Alright, well tell him I say hi. What do you want me to do?"

"We need three stories written for the morning. I'm writing one right now, and Lukas is writing from his dorm. Can you write the third one? The sound for it is in the folder on the server," Ryker says. I nod and go into my editing suite, shutting the door behind me.

I start to listen to the audio file which I realize is twenty minutes long. I hold in a groan as I think about transcribing twenty minutes worth of a boring interview about the changes coming to the airport in the town south of Northwich. Nevertheless, I listen to all of it and type everything up. I go to the printer and get the three pieces of paper I wrote. My eyes search the page for soundbites to include in the story. The problem with stories like this is the people we interview don't say anything of note; they simply state facts and go home. I need a good two or three pieces of audio to capture the listener's attention. Otherwise, I'll have a dry story full of facts people can easily read about online.

While I listen to the audio, I keep thinking about the two boys in the frat house. The only guys I've interacted extensively with at all this semester are voices I would have definitely recognized. Taylor's gruff and conceded tone isn't hard to miss and Drew would've recognized Finn in a heartbeat. Even Greenwood's trademark authoritative pitch wasn't present. I'm a bit angry at myself for having overlooked people taking pictures of me. Although, they could've taken them on their phones, and I wouldn't have noticed. The idea of strangers following me around 24/7 does scare me, but the thought of those paddles just hanging in that closet like trophies for all of these years freaks me out even more.

I don't look at the clock until my phone rings, and I see it's been an hour since I've arrived. Drew is calling me. I tap the 'Accept' button and put the phone to my ear.

"Hey hey roomie!" says Drew, slurring her words.

"Hey Drew. Are you good?" I ask her slowly, a small pit forming in my stomach.

Drew giggles, a sound that I've never heard come out of her mouth except for when she's around Finn.

"I'm fine," she drags out. "Hey, Kenni bailed. She's gotta study. I was callin' to see whatcha up to."

"I'm writing a story about the airport near here," I explain.

"Brooklyn, you're so talented." I snort and laugh at my intoxicated roommate. "Hey, did you know Dex plays music at the other radio station on campus?"

"I did not know that." I think about it for a second. "Wait, is he there with you right now?"

"Yeah Dex is here!" she confirms in a high-pitched voice. That pit drops to the floor.

"Drew, be careful," I warn. She blows air out through her lips.

"Don't be such a Nervous Nellie. I'm gonna be fine," she drunkenly promises.

"Alright. I should be home soon," I nervously assure her.

"Okie dokie. See ya!" Drew hangs up, and I put the phone down on the table. Something about the whole Dex situation doesn't sit right with me. Hell, I don't even know where the guy is from let alone what his intentions are. I decide I need to hurry up with writing my story and get home as soon as possible before anything unsavory happens.

I pull the best three sound bites I can find and edit them. My fingers fly across the keyboard as I throw together a story. It's definitely not my best, but I want to get home. The clock hits 9:50 as I put a period on the last sentence. I give it a quick-once over and then print it out.

"Done?" Ryker asks, pulling on his coat.

"Yeah." I put the story in Peter's mailbox, so he can read it in the morning then put on my jacket.

"Hey, uh, you want a ride? It's raining," Ryker offers. I pause, thinking it might be faster to walk rather than risk riding in Ryker's piece of junk. I decide a ride in any car is better than getting soaked in the downpour.

"Sure," I say. Ryker shuts down the computer I was using and turns off the lights to the newsroom. He waves to the kid sitting in the production booth up front and the two of us leave out of the front door. He holds open the door for me as I flip up my hood. It isn't raining that hard, but I'm sure it'll become worse as the night goes on.

"Who was that?" I ask, going to his car that's parked on the side of the building.

"Isaiah. He's a senior too. He's a good guy," Ryker summarizes. He rushes to his car and opens it with the little remote on his keychain. The two of us get into the car and out of the steady rain that's coming down. He adjusts himself and clears his throat, turning the car over so the engine revs up. I see his eyes nervously dart around.

"I live in Smith," I remind him.

"I remember," rushes Ryker as he backs up out of the driveway. The wipers whisk away the raindrops pounding against the windshield as the old car fights its way along the street. Focusing on anything besides Ryker at the moment is difficult. His jumpy manner is sort of scaring me. With every stop, he hits the brake so hard my chest bangs against my seatbelt.

"So, you aren't doing anything tonight?" I try to ask him calmly as I see a group of girls huddle underneath an umbrella while walking.

"I'm staying in. What about you?" he asks, looking out of the window as we stop at a red light.

"Well, my roommate is currently getting drunk with a guy," I say.

Ryker does a low whistle. "You better get home then," he says, clearly distracted. He turns his head to look at me and the streetlights combined with the red traffic light illuminate his face in an eerie way. For a brief moment, I see him contemplate kissing me. His lips slightly part, his eyes survey my face, and he leans in ever so slightly.

Now it feels like I'm going to vomit what with the pit in my stomach reaching a new level of low. I wedge myself into the corner between the seat and the door. "What?" I whisper to him, my breath coming in short.

"Nothing." Ryker's eyes still won't leave my face. I see his hand grip the steering wheel tighter. I shrink back against the cloth seat. I can hear my heart pound in my ears. I unbuckle myself and slowly go to leave the car.

"I can walk if you—"

"No!" Ryker snaps, locking the doors. He looks ragged and crazed in the light. "You're staying." I breathe harder. Every passing millisecond seems to wind Ryker tighter.

"Let me out," I demand. He doesn't move. The longer he stays still, the more he looks like a foreboding gargoyle perched at the entrance to a church. I've started to shake, but I can't discern whether I'm cold or fearing for my life. "Ryker, what's going on?" Ryker shakes his head and bites his bottom lip.

"I'm sorry," he finally relents. Something in my chest drops.

At that moment, a few things happen at the same time.

The traffic light turns green.

Ryker slams on the gas.
I scream.
Someone pulls my hair backwards.
A cloth comes over my nose and mouth.
When I inhale, the lights start to blur.
My body shuts down.

20

It's Ryker.
Ryker wants me dead.

When my eyes open, it takes my brain a second to process what I see.

I'm lying in a closet curled up in the fetal position. The set of doors in front of me is slightly cracked open so a sliver of light shines into the dusty closet. My head feels fuzzy and my body feels like it was been beaten before being thrown in here and forgotten. I deduce that I'm in the SHA house in one of the bedrooms on the top floor. I try to creep closer to the door, but find my hands are duct taped together. As disgusting as it sounds, the sweat on my skin from being nervous allows me to slip right out of it. I toss the tape to the side, unwind the tape from around my feet, and look directly into the light.

Then I hear voices.

"I guess I can't expect you to take a stand on what to do with her, Williams. You've been a weak leader from the beginning," accuses a familiar voice. When I get close enough to see out of the closet, my heart drops.

It's Taylor talking to none other than Ryker who has abandoned his flannel for the grey shirt he's wearing underneath it. Taylor looks like he's fuming as he stares Ryker down from across the room. As I look around at the brothers that I can see, I recognize James from Nate's frat standing behind Taylor next to a guy I don't know. A couple people away standing in the corner is the skinny scummy boy that was in my room yesterday. Dex is staring through his long locks at Ryker with contempt. The boys seem to be standing in a circle with Taylor and Ryker in the center like a boxing ring. The longer they stay silent, the more I can hear the rain hitting the rooftop. It would be calming in any other situation. Ryker's scoff at Taylor makes my eyes snap back to them.

"I have *not* been weak," Ryker defends.

"Yeah?" Taylor walks threateningly towards Ryker, but he doesn't budge. "Alright, so you've seen what that bitch has done. She wants to turn us in, get us all expelled, all for keeping something buried that should've been forgotten by now. And *you* want to let her go. Sounds damn weak to me."

"I don't want to let her go—"

"Oh, fuck off, Williams! You're not dedicated, *period.* Look." Taylor yanks up the sleeve of his black jacket to show Ryker something on his arm. I really have to squint, but I see the two lines I noticed on his arm are the bottoms of the number 97. "You see this? I've been nothing but committed to this fraternity. You do this as some sick tribute to a dead family member of yours."

"He's not dead. And you, you do it to tell your dad that you got into a real fraternity when in reality, you didn't!" Ryker snaps. "You're dedicated because you have to be for your father's sake. What's he going to do when he finds out that his jackass of a son isn't who he says he is?"

"Shut up," Taylor orders with another step forward. Ryker still doesn't move. "When am I going to be promoted from being your bitch, Williams? When's *that* going to happen?"

"I'm graduating this year. You can take the position of president then," Ryker says levelly. Taylor scoffs and shakes his head, taking a step towards Ryker so the two boys are about six feet apart.

"I don't want to wait until then," Taylor growls, his eyes matching a lion's. In an instant, he looks like he's got an idea, but he's clearly been thinking about it for days. "What about this? You leave *now* and I don't have to murder you in your sleep."

"Watch yourself, you psychopath. I'm still the leader," Ryker warns him in a low voice. Taylor looks like he's about to pounce when he seems to reconsider. He turns to the circle of boys and sighs.

"That's right, Ryker! You *are* the leader! And you say you're not weak so tell me: What do we do with the little bitch lying in the closet?" Taylor asks, turning smugly to Ryker. My stomach clenches and my breath catches in my throat. Ryker looks at the closet, and I shrink back as if I can blend into the woodwork. I swear I see a pained expression emerge briefly on Ryker's face as he looks at the door. If it's possible, Taylor becomes even more impatient. "*I said*, what do we do with the bitch, Williams?"

"We can't hurt her. It would be too suspicious." Ryker turns to the other brothers who are standing like statues observing the scene in front of them. They seem to have turned into robots and only speak when they're asked to. The rest of the time, they stand stock still, waiting to be summoned. "We can't be exposed again. We hurt her, she goes to the cops, and we're screwed.

You guys want to be found out?" Taylor shakes his head and crosses his arms.

"Just because *you* don't want to hurt that girl, doesn't mean *we* can't do something to her," Taylor snarls.

"I'll hurt her, I just—"

"Bullshit you will. What, you want to slap her on the cheek and send her home? She needs to die for what she knows, Williams. James has been calling her with warnings she won't listen to. She's gone to the damn cops about us. She's been asking for it, and you've been overlooking it for far too long." I roll my eyes at myself. *James was calling me.*

Ryker looks angrily confused. "I thought I said not to—"

"But see, they don't listen to you, Williams." Taylor says in a loud voice, gesturing around to all of the guys with his finger. "They know what you've done for the little rat." Ryker's eyebrows crease as the beginning of a troubling smile appears on Taylor's face.

"What?"

"We don't listen to a president who has forgotten the pledge," Taylor hisses.

"Okay, I don't know what the hell you're talking about," Ryker clearly lies, taking a step back.

"Confess, you sickening piece of shit. We know you've been helping the little bitch," growls Taylor. My heart plummets as does my jaw. Ryker looks confused.

"What?"

"You've been helping Brooklyn Perce with her investigation into our fraternity," Taylor challenges.

Ryker pauses in shock. "You're gonna accuse me of—"

"It's not an accusation if it's true," Taylor says, the corners of his mouth curling more and more upwards. Ryker makes a sound of disbelief and turns to the boys standing around them.

"You guys believe this shit?" Ryker asks the crowd. "He's lying to you!"

"I told you, they don't listen to you anymore!" Taylor says loudly over Ryker. Ryker turns back to Taylor, helpless. Taylor takes a few pondering steps towards his enemy. "What was it you said to her, again? Oh, that's right. 'Call me, I'll be there,'" Taylor says sweetly, the terrible smile now in full form. "What a *chivalrous* man you are, Williams." Ryker glares at Taylor, his lip twitching.

"I wanted to keep tabs on her, keep her trust. I didn't mean that," Ryker says through his teeth.

"Oh, but I think you did!" Taylor shouts. Ryker's words fail him as his facial expression proves his guilt. I hang my head and glance upwards at Ryker's defeated face as we both share in his hopelessness.

Taylor smiles like a snake who has strangled a mouse and opens his arms like he's presenting on a stage. "Look at that. Our *always loyal* leader Ryker Williams has betrayed us. So, it seems like he's no longer the president of the Sigma Eta Alpha fraternity. And *that*..." Taylor turns to Ryker and strolls towards him as Ryker fumes in his place. "Means I'm in charge."

"You prick," Ryker snarls.

"And as the former president, you know the cardinal rule, Williams. You either die with the secret or..." If it's possible, Taylor's smile grows. "It kills you." Taylor kicks

Ryker in the stomach which makes him drop to his knees as he coughs like a madman. Taylor jerks his chin at two guys standing behind Ryker who quickly pin him down. One of them grabs Ryker's wrists and twists them behind his back and the other yanks his hair backwards so he looks up at Taylor.

"James!" Taylor barks. James wakes up from his stupor and snaps to attention. "Give me something to swing at this jackass's head." James nods once and turns to the wall behind him which I can't see. James reappears with one of the SHA paddles from the closet in his hand. Taylor takes the wooden thing and flips it over in his hand, admiring it. He saunters over to Ryker who's struggling on the floor.

"You can't do this," Ryker hisses.

"I know, but the only guy who could stop me is on the floor," Taylor says with a fake pout. He grips the paddle like a baseball bat and smiles down at Ryker. I look around at the boys that I can see and none of them have moved. They seem perfectly content with watching the murder that's going to happen. I look at Dex who has shut his eyes, and then I look to James who is staring fully at the scene in front of him. The charismatic Delta Rho brother looks almost happy that Ryker will be killed. And am I better than them? I'm just going to sit in this closet while someone is killed.

This is insane.

"Anything you want to say, Williams?" Ryker just spits at Taylor's feet. Taylor chuckles and raises paddle high above his head, a maniacal glint in his eyes. Ryker shies away from the thing and braces for the blow. Taylor laughs to himself as his knuckles grow white from gripping the paddle.

WHOOSH.

"WAIT!" I scream, bursting out of the closet. I've startled most of the brothers, and in doing so, snapped them out of their trances. They all look at me, clearly stunned by the girl with the wild hair who just leapt out of the closet. I can hear the rain again as everything goes silent.

Taylor growls at me like an angry wolf, his paddle inches from Ryker's head. "I knew you were awake." He waves the wooden thing at me like he's scolding a little kid as he comes closer to me. "You're a tricky little thing, aren't you, Perce?"

"I'm full of surprises," I snarl.

"You really are." Taylor licks his lips and grins, although he bares his teeth more than he smiles. "Tricky, tricky little girl," he repeats to himself in a tone that makes the hairs on my neck stand up.

"How did you know I would come when Ryker texted?" I ask him, trying to stall Ryker's butchering.

Taylor smirks. "You trust him. And you of all people should know trust is a *bad* thing, especially in a position like yours." I look over to Dex who has opened his eyes and is intent on staring at the floor.

"Did you sic Dex on my roommate tonight?" I ask Taylor. When he doesn't say anything and just gives me that same infuriating smile, I take four steps forward and forcefully shove him backwards. The boys gasp and make a move to grab me, but Taylor stops them with a glare. "What did you do to Drew?" I ask in a stronger voice. Taylor turns to Dex who is trying to avoid eye contact with me.

"Tell her, Dex," Taylor orders. When Dex doesn't say anything, Taylor says louder, "*Speak, Dexter.*"

Dex softly clears his throat and looks at Taylor. He still refuses to look at me as he talks in a monotone. "I got the roommate drunk on purpose and started talking about the girl. The roommate said the girl was close to figuring out the truth. I contacted Ryker and agreed to have two boys wait in the back of his car until the time was right. And then we kidnapped the girl and brought her here." Dex sounds like he's reciting from a drilling manual.

"You're a miserable piece of shit," I insult. Dex shrinks back into the corner where he came from.

"We're all terrible in our own way. Even you, Perce." I turn to Taylor who looks proud of himself.

"I'm not like you," I say. His nose twitches in annoyance and his smile slips slightly.

"Oh really? You think you're so *special* just because you figured out what a hundred men couldn't. You have something to prove which makes you do stupid things, like not caring about the safety of those people you call your friends. Your arrogance is what makes you horrible, Perce. Just like me" Taylor's proud grin is back, and it makes me take a step away from him. "At least I own up to it." He turns to Ryker who's still being held by the two frat brothers, a disgusted look coming over his face. "This one, not so much." Taylor reaches out to grab Ryker by the throat.

"Don't!" I blurt, looking down at Ryker. Taylor turns back to me, eyes lit with rage.

"You don't want me to hurt him? Adorable," Taylor snickers through his teeth. He turns away from me and acts like he's walking away when he turns around and swiftly hits me in the stomach with the wooden paddle. The blow knocks all of the air out of me, and I stumble back against the wall to steady myself. Taylor throws the paddle aside and picks me up by my jacket, slamming me against the wall. My head snaps back against the crumbling drywall, and I let out a scream. "You wanna take his place?" he jeers softly with the little smile. I see Jason and all the other guys except Ryker stare at me with neutral expressions as Taylor drops me to the ground and I collapse in a heap. Quickly, I scuttle to a sitting position and prop myself against the wall. Taylor aims a kick at my chest which I dodge but end up getting my ear punched instead. The hit whips my head to the side and leaves a small crack in the wall. Taylor kicks me in the side, so I fall to the left and a cloud of dust erupts from the baseboards.

"Taylor, stop!" Ryker says in a desperate tone. Taylor whirls around in a rage, the black coat he's wearing flaring out around him. Ryker stares up at Taylor with a defiant expression as Taylor's psychotic hyena smile emerges. He does this high-pitched laugh that makes my blood curdle and my stomach churn. I stay sitting against the wall, staring up at Taylor through my tangled hair. I feel my nose start to bleed. A little trickle of blood makes its way down my face and begins to dye the ends of my hair. Taylor looks at me and smiles harder, proud of his work. His maniacal laugh turns into a chuckle.

"I knew your dumb ass would fall in love with her," he finally smirks.

"What are you talking about?" I say breathlessly, pretending like this is news to me.

"Don't listen—AH!" Ryker yelps as he gets hit in the chest by one of the guys holding him. My eyes dart from Ryker to Taylor and back again.

"Perce," pouts Taylor pitifully, crouching down and putting his hand under my chin, so I have to look down my nose at him. "You were so consumed in figuring out your little mystery that you didn't see, so let me spell it out for you. This asshole has had a thing for you from the moment you walked into that radio station." I see Ryker hang his head from out of the corner of my eye. The words coming out of Taylor's mouth make me want to spit in his face.

"You're lying," I say instinctually.

Taylor scoffs. "Don't believe me, eh?" Taylor walks over to Ryker and violently kicks him in the chest. Ryker coughs out blood onto the floor of the house before his chin is tilted upwards by the toe of Taylor's black boot. The two men look at each other and the tension between their eyes is horrifying. "Tell her Ryker. Tell her how you've been planning to break up her and her pathetic boyfriend." Now, *that's* news to me. Ryker breathes heavily through his nose as blood starts to seep out from in between his lips. Taylor's kick must've caught him in the mouth.

"Ryker?" I say expectantly. He looks at me in desperation, and his eyes meet mine. I quietly sigh as I realize his loving gaze. He's looking at me with all the care in the world, like how Nate did that night on the roof. I feel this tight fist wrap around my intestines and squeeze until I'm overcome with the urge to throw up.

"Brooklyn..." he whimpers helplessly. Taylor laughs with a sort of sadistic glee. He saunters back over to me and sighs nostalgically.

"I'm really going to enjoy killing you, Perce. And you know what's going to make it a thousand times better? We're going to make Ryker watch."

"What!" Ryker shrieks as the boys drag him backwards and stand him up. His hands are still behind his back as the brothers struggle to hold onto him. I try to scurry out of Taylor's reach, but he takes me by the shirt, pulling me upright, and pinning me to the wall.

"Remember how I said I wanted to strangle you?" Taylor asks, his face inches from mine. His breath smells like he just ate mulch and the way his teeth look doesn't do much to disprove that theory. My heartbeat is the only thing I can hear, and my massive eyes are threatening me with tears. I bite my lip as I concentrate on not letting them stream down my cheeks. I make eye contact with Ryker again whose face is the perfect picture of anguish. Meanwhile, Taylor's perverse smile is only growing wider. *He's really going to do this.*

"I promise I won't tell anyone about anything," I whisper, finally breaking down. "*Please* let me go."

"Wish I could. You got yourself into this…" Taylor bares his teeth. "Now, get yourself out." I get one last breath in before Taylor takes me by the throat and immediately starts to squeeze. I try to defend myself, but he's standing on my feet, so I can't knee him in the crotch. Prying his hands off of my neck doesn't work either so my arms drop to my sides and start to shake. I begin to choke and everything I hear sounds muffled. My hands search the wall behind me, praying for some sort of weapon. My body starts to tense up as the lack of oxygen gets to me. I start to sweat profusely. Taylor's face is starting to blur, and the word is turning into a black and white dot painting.

"Goodbye Brooklyn," Taylor snarls as my eyes starts to close. My fingers stop feeling the wall, and they're about to give up when my palm brushes a nail. With every last ounce of strength in my wilting body, I rip the

217

rusted nail out of the wall and whip it across Taylor's chest, catching some of his face with the tip at the end. He roars in pain and frustration and releases me. Air rushes into my lungs as I take a ragged breath. The boys are stunned. Ryker takes advantage of their surprise by elbowing the guys holding him in the stomach. Another brother tries to take Ryker by the neck from behind, but Ryker aims a backwards kick that catches the guy in the crotch. Two guys and James try to come after me, but I dodge one of them so he runs into the wall. James looks at me with no emotion and puts me in a headlock, starting my choking cycle all over again. I contort my hand to grab onto his face and I begin to sink my fingers into his eyes. James roars in pain. Ryker punches another guy as James lets go of me. A kick to the face knocks him out for good. A brother is tending to Taylor who has a gash that's seeping blood from the nail going across his chest and what looks like his lower lip. Taylor's head snaps up from looking at his wound. He emits a guttural growl that makes my eyes widen and my legs freeze.

"Run!" Ryker grabs me by the wrist and pulls me towards the steps. We get down to the first floor of the house, and I go for the window, but Ryker shakes his head and pulls me towards the basement. "The tunnel."

"Let me go!" I yell, ripping my wrist out of his grasp.

"I'm trying to help you!" Ryker shouts. I hear Taylor and the other boy thundering down the stairs. With a small reluctant sigh, I run for the basement, Ryker trailing close behind. There's a second when I think we're home free but, of course, we run into more problems.

I trip down the last step and fall right into someone's arms which lock around my chest like a vice. I look up in fear at a guy wearing a black hoodie and try to escape his grasp, but it's no use. He has me.

"Tie her," orders Taylor from the top of the stairs. I turn around with difficulty and stare at Taylor who slowly walks down the stairs as my wrists are tied behind my back and I'm dragged backwards. My ankles are bound as a scratchy rope is put around my neck. A noose. *Oh no, no, no, no.* My heart pounds so hard I think it might burst. I see Ryker has been subdued as two guys drag him backwards, his head hanging limply from his neck.

"Aren't you proud of me? I got myself out of it up there," I gibe.

"Very proud," Taylor says sarcastically. "Scared, Perce?"

"No," I lie. The psychopath is handed the paddle from a brother. He smirks.

"Liar." I hold back a scream as he swings the paddle like a bat at my stomach. The place where the wood hits stings then burns like hell. He whacks me across the chest so now my entire front is bruised. Taylor snickers as he hits the back of my knees. My legs automatically crumple, but the noose doesn't give. When I sink to the ground, I start to choke. The rope digs into my neck, pulling me up towards the ceiling. I quickly try to get back to my feet, but Taylor pushes me backwards. My head slams into the cinderblock behind me and I feel dizzy. My body wants so badly to let go, but I force it to hold on. Taylor grabs my face with his hand.

"Scream, Perce," Taylor orders before hitting me with the paddle across the stomach again. "Scream!" He punches me across the face, and I finally allow myself to start to cry.

"STOP!" I yell, tears streaming down my face.

"That's a girl!" Taylor approves with glee, clearly enjoying every second of this.

"Please stop," I relent, blood pouring out of my nose.

"Giving up so soon?" Taylor asks like he's talking to a baby. "Too bad I'm like you." He hits me on the side before coming dangerously close to my ear. I feel his hot breath on my bloody skin as he hisses, "I don't know when to stop." He aims the paddle at my head, and I wait for the last thing I'll ever feel when I hear someone burst into the basement. The boys and I turn to look at the newcomers. When I can finally see them, I try to stifle a gasp of relief.

There's Drew, Nate, and Finn standing in the closet covered with dirt from the tunnel. Drew and Finn are standing on opposite sides of Nate. Taylor laughs as he looks at the three of them.

"Shocking," Taylor deadpans, putting his hand underneath my chin and shaking his head. "Look who's here to save the day." He slides my boyfriend a nasty glare.

"Get away from her," Nate orders in a scarily serious tone, taking a step forward.

Taylor drops his hand and turns back to Nate. "Always the hero, aren't we, Stevenson?"

"Let Brook go," Nate says in the same dangerous tone.

"You're gonna make me?" Taylor questions. Nate, realizing he has no weapon, glances to the corner where the rusted coat of arms sits. Swiftly, he pulls on the handle of one of the swords and it comes loose, a few sparks flying out of it. Even he looks surprised. I see Drew roll her eyes and shake her head as though even she knows this would only happen to Nate. The smug grin on Taylor's face fades, but it's quickly picked up by Nate's.

"Yeah," he says with the cocky smile. Nate takes another step forward. "Let her go." Nate takes an abrupt step forward which makes five boys step forward in the defense of their leader. Taylor smirks.

"That wouldn't be fun," he says like the Joker.

"What would be?" Nate spits, tired of Taylor's game.

Taylor smiles. He pauses as the boys vibrate with anticipation in their spots. Finn's hands make fists at his sides and Drew poses her fingers like claws, her long fingernails at the tips. Nate grips the hilt of the sword with two hands as he sees the glint in Taylor's eye "Get them." The pack of boys springs into action, attacking my friends with the veracity of wolves. I hear Drew scream as she's almost choked, see Finn punch out Jason as he runs at Drew, and Nate is hacking away with the sword all while Taylor starts to run up the stairs.

"NATE!" I scream. Once I have his attention, I look to Taylor who has almost made it to the top of the stairs. Nate runs after Taylor and swipes at his ankles. The sword's blade catches Taylor's black jacket which makes him trip, his face taking the brunt of the fall.

Drew makes her way over to me and starts to undo the rope around my ankles and wrists as Finn continues to fight off the murderous boys. Once I slip the noose off of my neck, I can finally breathe easy. Drew turns to help Finn, but I turn to Ryker who's still passed out in the corner. His helpless body was just tossed against the cinderblock. Something in me wants to leave him there. Serves him right for wanting to kill me. But a larger part of me can't see him hurt. Drew tugs on my wrist and I shake my head.

"I can't just leave him," I tell her. Drew nods in understanding. Finn lets out a scream, and Drew's head whips around.

"Finn!" Drew shrieks, letting me go and running over to him, punching a guy square in the nose.

I crouch down on the floor next to Ryker and check to make sure his heart is still beating. All of a sudden, I hear the jarring sound of metal hitting metal. Everything stops as we turn to see that Nate has tried to bring the sword down on Taylor's head, but Taylor has found the other. He's holding it horizontally above his head perpendicular to Nate's, their eyes locked.

"Try harder, Stevenson," Taylor spits under his breath, forcing Nate down the stairs by shoving his sword away.

I turn back to Ryker and shake his shoulder. I look desperately behind me, but Finn and Drew are still swinging at the last two standing boys, the others passed out on the ground. I see Drew land a punch on Dex, which I know must feel good. My hand keeps shaking Ryker's body.

"Ryker. Ryker, c'mon," I plead. The clanging of metal keeps ringing behind me, but I keep urging him to wake up.

"BROOKLYN, TURN AROUND!" Drew screams.

Before I can so much as move my head, I'm slammed into the concrete wall by Taylor and pinned there by the dulled rusty sword to my neck. I try to force him off of me, but he's too strong. Taylor presses the dull blade harder onto my neck and I start to choke.

"Good," he hisses. I ram my knee into his crotch, and he crumples. The sword goes flying into the depths of the basement. Nate and the suddenly conscious Ryker grab Taylor from behind and drag him backwards. I put my foot on his chest and stamp down, taking all air out of him. When he looks up at me with hatred, I give him one of his sick smiles.

"Good," I snarl. That's when I lay into his face with my fists. I don't care what I break as I punch him with ferocity. He screams and cries out in pain, but that only makes me want to punch him more. I can feel the terrified stares of Drew, Finn, Nate, and Ryker as they just let me hit and claw at Taylor's face. Eventually, Ryker pulls me backwards by the shoulders. I think he says my name, but I can't be sure. I'm numb to everything. It feels like I've been mutilating Taylor for hours.

Nate points the tip of the sword in Taylor's face as my boyfriend and I look down on the snake. Chest heaving, Taylor chuckles like a maniac. The blood coming out of his mouth and nose splashes out at me as he laughs. He lies back on the floor with a sigh and looks at me through his one good eye, the other damaged by me raking my fingernails across his face.

"Kill me," Taylor says simply. Ryker's grip on my shoulders tightens as if he knows I'm thinking about honoring Taylor's request. "*Kill me.*" He almost sounds like he's begging for it.

Nate shakes his head. "I'm not crazy like you," says Nate.

Taylor chuckles, exposing his bloody teeth. The sound of his low maniacal laugh makes my blood run cold. "You're not," says Taylor. He slides his eyes over to look directly at me. I freeze. "But she is." I shrink backwards a bit, but don't say a thing. "You're just as cold and calculating as me, Perce. Somewhere in you, you want to kill me. But you won't." Taylor's chest goes up and down as he laughs to himself. "And I want to kill you! But I won't. So we'll keep playing this game until one of us is dead. And you *will* die. Someone like you will die a horrible and painful death all because she stuck her nose where it didn't belong."

21

About a half hour later, I'm sitting wrapped in a blanket in the back of an open ambulance trying to avoid the little bit of snow falling from the sky. After all, it is an early November morning in Central New York. Why not have snow decorating the creepy fraternity house as all of the brothers are put in handcuffs in front of it?

Taylor has a cop car all to himself. The dried blood on his face seems to be freezing to his skin as he stands in the cold. He throws me a dirty look before he's shoved inside of the car and the door slams.

I'm so tired. The past couple of hours have drained me, although I'm not sure I want to go to sleep. If I do, I'll probably see Taylor torturing me or Ryker trapping me in his car. I'm already afraid to close my eyes for longer than it takes me to blink despite my eyelids being tugged down by the will to nap. Every little movement going on in front of me makes me jump. Whenever a car door is slammed, my muscles tense as though the sound will make its way over and punch me. I'm so preoccupied with trying to take in the scene that I don't notice the paramedic walking over.

"Hey hon, how are you feeling?" she asks kindly. All I can do is grimace and nod. She understands I don't want to talk and takes my blood pressure in silence.

I watch Nate talk to a cop, the sword still in his hand like it somehow became fused to his palm. Finn has his arm wrapped around Drew who still seems to be in shock from everything that has happened. They sit in a different ambulance and stare at a spot on the pavement. I hear the paramedic make a sound of approval as she rips the Velcro from my arm. She takes note of my blood pressure then leaves.

"Hey," says a familiar voice. After wincing slightly, I turn to my left and see Ryker. The white snow is collecting on his dark hair as he looks down at me. I look down at my lap, determined to stay silent. Ryker sighs. "Are you doing okay?" I swallow and don't say a word, although rage is quickly building inside of me. "Look, Brooklyn, I'm sorry for…all of this. You heard me in there. I tried to stop them. I didn't want anything to happen to you because—"

"Because you liked me," I finish angrily, looking up at him. Ryker looks guilty as all hell. "You would've been fine killing anyone else so long as it wasn't me."

"That's not true," he says with no malice in his voice.

"Bullshit," I say, shaking my head and smiling in disbelief. "Ryker, do you realize what you've done to me? You lead me to believe I was your friend. And then I'm kidnapped in your car and wake up in a closet, only to get beaten, and for what? My *curiosity?*"

"I know. Brooklyn, I'm—"

"Sorry? If you're sorry you wouldn't have done this." I bite my bottom lip, becoming more infuriated by the second. "You made my roommate trust you. You made me trust you…" Ryker crouches down so his face is below mine. He's on the verge of tears. He takes my hands in his, and I don't pull them away because he's warm and I'm freezing. Ryker starts to handle my fingers like he's memorizing how my hand feels in his. "Answer me this." Ryker pauses and looks up at me. "Did you really want to get between me and Nate?"

"No. I want you to be happy." Ryker looks over at Nate who's still talking to the police. "And if he makes you happy…" He glances down at the ground. "I thought that by staying, I could protect you, but clearly…" Ryker looks into my eyes, and I can see the pain he's trying to hold back. He scoffs at himself and looks over his shoulder at Nate. "I'm an idiot, Brooklyn. And I'm so incredibly sorry for everything."

I shake my head. "You should be." Swallowing, I take my hand out of his grasp. "I hope you're locked up until you're fifty. Better yet, I hope you die in there."

Ryker looks distraught. "You don't mean that."

"Yeah I do. I do, Ryker, I *really* do," I say, nodding vigorously. Ryker clears my hair out of my face and leaves his hand on my cheek. We look into each other's eyes, his containing love, mine containing contempt. "Go," I whisper, moving my face so his hand slips away. He swallows as the sound of crunching footsteps approach us.

"Ryker, the cops want to talk to you," Nate says in a stern voice. Ryker nods and gets up, smiling at me.

"Goodbye Brooklyn," says Ryker, walking away backwards so he can see me. Once Ryker passes Nate, he bumps Nate's shoulder which makes Nate rolls his eyes.

"Great guy," Nate says in a monotone as he sits in the ambulance next to me. I lean my head on his shoulder and he puts his arm around me. "What did he want to say?"

"Nothing important." We watch as Ryker is pushed into the back of a cop car in the same manner as Taylor. Ryker gives me a longing glance and a grimace before his head is put inside and the door is shut.

"How did you know where I was?" I ask Nate, not taking my eyes off of the car.

"When you didn't come home for three hours, we knew something was wrong," Nate says. "You're lucky Drew called Finn and me. Otherwise…" Nate shivers. "I don't want to think about otherwise."

"Thank you," I say, kissing him on the cheek. "For everything."

"You're welcome," he says, kissing me on the lips. "For everything."

"And the sword," I say. Nate raises his eyebrows. "Nice touch."

"Thanks. I'm surprised it even came loose." He admires the thing in his hand then looks to me with a smile. "I'm so happy you're safe."

"I'm happy I'm alive," I say truthfully.

"That too," Nate says. He kisses the top of my head. I see Drew and Finn walking over to us, his arm around her. Drew gives me a huge hug when she reaches us. She's shaking and I can't tell if it's from shock or the cold. Finn hugs me when Drew decides to let go.

"I don't even know how to thank you. All of you," I say.

"Thank Kenni. She's the one who called all of them," says Drew, gesturing to the various police cars and ambulances.

"But I would've been choked to death if it wasn't for you guys coming in," I say.

"With excellent timing," Finn adds. I look at Finn and grimace.

"I know you hate frats, and I'm sorry but—"

Finn holds up a hand to stop me. "It's okay. You figured out who killed my dad. I thought I owed you one," Finn says with a small smile.

I glance at Drew, clearly confused. "How does he—"

"I told him everything on the way over," Drew jokes.

I wince. "Sorry I kept digging into your life," I apologize. Finn chuckles, shakes his head, and puts an arm around Drew.

"I'm not happy about it, but I'm just glad you're okay." Finn clears his throat. "Brook, did you ever figure out what happened to my mom?" He sounds like he's trying not to be interested.

"I think she might be missing. I'm sorry," I say. Finn nods and looks disappointed. Drew leans her head on his arm and gives him an apologetic hug.

"Brooklyn Perce," says a snide voice. Finn and Drew move over to make way for Officer Greenwood. The sun is a few hours away from coming up, but he's still chewing gum. "How are you feeling?"

"Shaken up, but I'll be alright," I sigh. Nate takes my hand and squeezes it reassuringly.

Greenwood nods. "Good, good." He looks at my friends. "All three of you deserve some praise. You helped catch some criminals. Well done," Greenwood praises. Then his eyes rest on me. "And you." My stomach clenches as I think of the cruel words that will come out of his mouth. "Your tenacity almost got you killed. Congratulations. You should be proud of your investigation." I smile as the corners of Greenwood's mouth turn upwards.

"Thank you, Officer." It's the first time I've truly meant something I've said to him.

"Giving credit where credit is due is important. Even if it is a girl who lies a bit to get what she wants," Greenwood admits. I share a tight smile with Nate. "We'll need statements from each of you soon. You've got a lot of questions to answer."

"What's there to say besides 'there was a murderous bitter group of boys on campus'?" Nate says.

"More than you'd think." Greenwood looks Nate up and down and smirks when he sees the sword. "Are you fencing later or something?"

All of us chuckle and Nate shakes his head. "No Sir." He offers it to Greenwood who gingerly takes it from him. The officer checks his watch and sighs. "It's almost four in the morning though. Why don't you all get some sleep? I will be in touch."

"Sleep sounds wonderful," Drew says weakly. All of us smile at her.

"See you in the morning, Officer," I say to Greenwood. He nods and claps me on the shoulder.

"Good work, kid." With that, Greenwood walks away.

"You think *he's* going to question us?" asks Nate when the officer is out of earshot.

"Nah. Someone more important than him is going to be doing that," I say.

Drew yawns. "Can we find out who that is tomorrow? I'm tired as hell." She looks to Finn with big begging eyes. "Carry me up the stairs?"

"No," Finn says. He suddenly sweeps her off of her feet and starts to carry her away. Drew and Finn are both laughing as they trudge to the back stairs. Nate and I get up from sitting, and I put the blanket around him as well. We walk in tandem. and I enjoy the feeling of finally being able to walk without fear of being watched. Although, I still feel as though something might pop out of the trees at any moment.

As our shoes make tracks in the accumulating snow, we make our way up to our dorm. It's snowing harder now than it was before, so much so that the little flakes catch my eyelashes and refuse to let go. I pull the blanket up over our heads to shield our eyes. Nate chuckles as we reach the front of my building.

"God, it's freezing," he says after I take the blanket off from around him. He looks up at the building. "Mind if I crash in your room tonight?"

"Why can't you walk the extra thirty steps to your dorm?" I ask him playfully.

Nate bites his lip and smiles. "Because the girls in this building are cuter," he says. I snort and then giggle. "Not you of course. Other girls."

"Right," I say, smiling broadly.

Nate gently puts his hands on my waist, and I try not to jump. "I'm so proud of you." He softly kisses me, but even when his lips touch mine, I slightly flinch. I take a second to look into his fiery amber eyes and thank whoever's out there that I'm alive to see them. "Love you."

"I love you too, Nate," I say. I take his hand and we go up the three steps to my building. I fumble at the doorway to get my R.U.I.D. out, but I manage to swipe into Smith. With one last look out into the darkness, I let the door slam shut behind me and walk into my home.

Made in the USA
Monee, IL
16 May 2020

30852107R10136